Briarfield Lane Collection

Stephanie A. Wilder

Briarfield Lane Collection

ISBN 979-8-3303-6274-5 (print)

Coming Home and *A Place to Land*
With New Epilogue

Coming Home

1

L *ord, please stop this man from calling the police on me.*

"Sir, a wellness check really isn't necessary," Harbor Wilson pleaded with God and with her very patient but very annoyed rideshare driver, Stanley.

Stanley's bulging brown eyes glared at Harbor through the rearview mirror. He methodically tapped chunky fingers on the steering wheel. "Lady, I think it is. I could have picked up two more fares by now," Stanley said. He turned to face her. "Look, I'm a patient man, but I got two kids in college, a nine-year-old who needs braces, and a wife who couldn't spell work if I put the letters right in front of her face. So, I gotta go."

Harbor groaned. It had only been fifteen minutes since Stanley and his immaculately maintained black sedan rolled up to her destination...137 Briarfield Lane. What's a mere fifteen minutes among friends? Or virtual strangers.

Lord, am I holding this man hostage?

With that realization, Harbor forced her size seven, fire engine red sneakers to move from the safety of Stanley's sturdy floor mats to an awaiting curb. She was a big girl, and she could do this. Right?

Harbor bit her lower lip. She looked at Stanley, gave an apologetic grin, and sighed. Her gaze shifted to the two-story, brick mini mansion with the neatly trimmed lawn just steps away from the safety of her rideshare and patient Stanley. If everyone in her life exhibited patience like Stanley, maybe Harbor would not be inclined to hold a stranger and his car hostage because she didn't want to face whatever was waiting for her in her childhood home.

Stanley cleared his throat, which had the effect of shocking Harbor out of her ill-advised trip down memory lane. "I hate to do this to you, ma'am, but I'm gonna have to count you down like I do my youngest," Stanley warned.

He waved his seen-better-days flip-phone over the seat. "Then, I gotta call someone. Ten...."

This bit of information jolted Harbor out of her self-imposed confinement. She threw up the timeout sign.

"No need to be rash, Stanley," Harbor's tone oozed with compliance. "And we certainly don't need to involve the authorities. I promise all I need is." The last few words of Harbor's impromptu speech were unceremoniously cut off.

"Five...four," Stanley said as he flashed each number with callused hands that screamed of a hard-working man with better things to do than babysit a grown woman with unresolved family issues and a tendency to choose flight over fight.

Harbor's "family issues" came packaged in the form of an always impeccably dressed and socially refined woman named Elizabeth "Lizzie" Wilson...Harbor's one and only mother.

To a world outside of 137 Briarfield Lane, Harbor's mother exuded a gentility that could only be described as uniquely southern. Elizabeth's hospitality knew no bounds...except when it came to her oldest daughter. As beautiful as her mother appeared on the outside, the woman lying within could become cold and detached in an instant.

Before Harbor found herself entangled in the depths of her tumultuous relationship with her mother, she dug in her fifth pocket for the emergency cash she kept on hand. Keeping patient Stanley from earning a living doing what he did seemed like as good of an emergency as anything else. She placed a fifty in Stanley's palm.

"I appreciate you," Harbor offered in a voice as close to "I'm sorry for holding you hostage" as she could muster.

Stanley's eyes shined with delight for the first time since he'd picked Harbor up at Norfolk International Airport. "Thank you, ma'am," Stanley replied.

His delight made Harbor genuinely smile.

She stepped out of the car onto the sidewalk and stared at the house in front of her. *It's just a week, Harbor. You can do this for a week*, Harbor reassured herself. She didn't believe a word of it, but she had to try.

Stanley popped the trunk. He was at her side in a flash, holding her overstuffed, steel-gray luggage. Stanley parked the luggage beside Harbor on the sidewalk. They stood silently, taking in the grander of the home before them.

Columns on either side of the grand porch stood at attention, like royal guards protecting the Wilson Estate. The lovely, gilded cage was a place she could have walked away from and never returned, but for a request from the one person Harbor could never say no to.

"This is some house," Stanley stated almost in reverence. "Can't imagine anything inside a place like this could be all that bad."

Harbor stifled the urge to roll her eyes. If Stanley only knew.

She grasped the handle of her luggage and set it in motion. "Let's hope not," Harbor yelled over her shoulder.

For the rest of her short journey up the walk to the house, Harbor kept her eyes focused on her target. If she allowed herself the luxury of looking back at Stanley, even for a moment, her next stop would be back to the airport and to the comfort of her one-bedroom slice of peace and tranquility in Atlanta.

***

Before Harbor could give the angelic-shaped knocker a few good taps, the massive oak door flew open. The anxious breath Harbor held in her throat since she'd landed in Norfolk slowly released as her gaze connected with her longtime ally...Amelia Livingston. Ms. Amelia served lovingly as the Wilson family's housekeeper for nearly thirty years. To Harbor and everyone else blessed to know the feisty, one-of-a-kind creation, Amelia Livingston was an angel in disguise. For Harbor, Ms. Amelia held a place in her heart reserved for a beloved nana or granny. She was just that special.

Amelia's petite frame enveloped Harbor in a fierce hug. The sweet woman, with a vibrant cocoa complexion, grasped her baby girl's shoulders, giving Harbor a discerning once-over.

"Baby girl, you look like you're losing weight," Amelia stated flatly. She tugged at the waistband of Harbor's stonewashed skinny jeans. "I can't have you falling off."

Harbor laughed and pulled Amelia in for another embrace. "I'm perfectly healthy, Ms. Amelia. Thank you very much."

Amelia rolled her eyes and huffed. "Tell me anything."

Before Harbor could respond, the woman hovering between seventy and seventy-five, no one knew or dared to ask her actual age, marched toward the kitchen with a confident stride. Harbor placed her luggage just inside the foyer and fell in line like a baby duckling following mama duck across the pond. Dutifully complying with Ms. Amelia's unspoken "request," Harbor kept in step. The woman was a force of nature and best be respected; Harbor inwardly laughed.

At some point in this experiment called life, Harbor would dig into why she literally fell in step with Ms. Amelia, no questions asked, but challenged her mother's significance in her life. If Harbor had her say, those moments of familial introspection would happen somewhere far, far down the road if they happened at all.

Harbor didn't know what would happen in the next seconds and minutes after she and Elizabeth finally laid eyes on each other after a five-year hiatus. So, she determined within herself to soak up every ounce of love Ms. Amelia generously lavished upon her and to unapologetically gobble up every ounce of the home cooked meal coming her way.

Cooking did not come easy for Harbor, so her stove and oven were for emergency use only. Thankfully, with all the culinary delights woven in and around Atlanta, Harbor did not have to suffer through eating her own disastrous creations.

Harbor sighed when she walked into the kitchen, which resembled a space a world-class chef would undoubtedly approve of. The space held a ten-foot island, standard and walk-in refrigerators, and smart appliances. The creature comforts she had accepted as a child and despised as a know-it-all teen and young adult were all a part of what made this space her home.

At that moment, Harbor finally realized she was actually home. "Help, Lord," she prayed, walking across the kitchen to take a seat at a cozy table near a window, facing the lake. Everyone in the house knew that corner of the kitchen was for Amelia's special use. Entering her space without express permission was a risk no one dared to take...except Harbor. From the time she could walk, Harbor always had open access to Amelia's cozy, carved-out space and never questioned why. It was just one of those gifts she accepted as a little wink from heaven during her sometimes up, most times down, growing up years.

The aroma from the steaming bowl of beef stew and plate of flaky biscuits made Harbor groan. She gave a quick prayer of thanks, and dug in. Amelia placed two cups of mint tea on the table and took a seat.

Neither woman spoke for several minutes as Harbor scooped up the last of her gravy with the remaining piece of biscuit.

Amelia took a sip of her tea. "Baby girl, if I didn't know any better, I'd think you ain't had a decent meal since you left." She nodded her head as if confirming her theory.

Harbor leaned back in her seat, both hands flat against her over-stuffed tummy. "I eat," she said quickly. That sounded lame to her own ears, so she knew Amelia was not fooled. "Okay, I eat when I remember to eat." Harbor tossed up her hands in mock surrender.

Amelia stood and took Harbor's bowl and plate to the sink. "Well, I can't do a thing about what you do or don't eat in Atlanta." She did a grand flourish with her hands. "But you will eat when you're in Amelia's space."

That is not a request, Harbor thought with not even a smidge of apprehension. Ms. Amelia Livingston could throw down in the kitchen. Harbor had enough good sense to fill her tummy and her soul, at least for the next week, with what it had been missing.

"Yes, ma'am." Harbor took another sip of her tea and then walked the cup and saucer to the sink. She handed the fine China to Ms. Amelia. Harbor locked eyes with her lifelong confidant. She blurted out, "Is she home?"

Amelia waved a dismissive hand. "I ain't nobody's keeper but my own. You know your mother. She'll get home when she gets home."

At those words, Harbor was relieved and disappointed all in the span of a moment. Coming face to face with her mother after five years of only minimal contact would at best be challenging and, at worst, be...the worst. Why did the thought of being in her mother's presence drive Harbor through the range of every emotional high and low on the feelings scale?

Harbor plucked a much too large oatmeal cookie from a glass container on the counter. She savored the chewy goodness of her childhood for probably too long of a moment. "I missed these." She sighed.

Amelia grasped Harbor's hand. "Just say the word, and I'll have a dozen baked and ready to mail to you once a week."

Harbor laughed. "Maybe every other week." She tossed the last bit of the delicious delicacy in her mouth.

Amelia winked. "We'll see." She gave Harbor another long look like she was trying to memorize her face before she said, "I got some laundry and dusting to do."

Harbor rolled her eyes. She doubted anything like dust would dare make itself at home in Ms. Amelia's space. 137 Briarfield Lane may have been the Wilson family's home, but Ms. Amelia ran the massive space exactly how she wanted. No one, not even Elizabeth, had a thing to say about it.

On her way out of the kitchen, Amelia said, "Get yourself all settled in while I get to my work. I'll text you when your mama gets here." She winked and made her way out of the kitchen.

Harbor peeked around the corner to ensure Ms. Amelia was good and on her way before she plucked another cookie from the jar.

"How did I live without these for so long?" Harbor mumbled as she took a giant bite and wrapped the remaining cookie in a paper towel before heading upstairs.

She decided to leave her luggage just where she'd parked it...at the front door. Elizabeth would have a dignified fit if the luggage sullied the ambiance of the expertly decorated entrance, Harbor thought. But she didn't care. At least, that was the line she had been feeding herself for the last five years. Somehow, Harbor knew her mother's opinion meant more to her than just about anything, which was a real drag.

Making her way up the spiral staircase, Harbor acknowledged the pictures of her past and present family members that made the journey toward the family rooms with her. A 1918 photograph of her great-great-grandparents, Clarence, and Katrina Wilson, took center stage. Harbor always loved to look at the stately-looking couple in their early twentieth-century finery. Although she would never truly know them, these were her people, and she was proud of her heritage.

A wedding photo of her mother and father and photos of both sets of grandparents also lined the wall for the journey upstairs.

There were four bedrooms on the second floor. Harbor's room was the first room just off the staircase. She always wondered why her parents would give their rebellious child the room with the easiest escape route. Sneaking out on a Friday night was almost anticlimactic but for Amelia's occasional teen-radar, catching Harbor in the act.

Harbor's hand hovered over her doorknob. Silly, but she almost wanted to ask permission before entering. "Get a grip, Girl," Harbor chided herself before opening the door.

She opened the door and gasped. The room looked like a shrine to her former self. Posters of eighties and nineties R&B bands lived on the wall above her bed. Her teddy bear, Theodore Goodnight, was placed in the center of her bed. The fluffy fellow sported the fancy tuxedo and bow tie he wore when Ms. Amelia gave him to Harbor for her fifteenth birthday. As a tenth grader, Harbor thought the silly bear was a lame gift. That was before she'd realized holding on to Mr. Goodnight helped her to relax and get a decent night's rest.

Harbor stepped over the threshold of her room, ran to the bed, and jumped on it, causing Theodore to fly in the air and land in her arms. She squeezed him as tightly as she could. Maybe it was Harbor's imagination, but Theodore seemed to give her a little squeeze back. Okay, she knew she was trippin', but seeing the old guy again made her heart smile.

Harbor looked at the shades of pink patchwork quilt on her bed with matching pillows. It was the same pattern on her bed the day she'd left, but the quilt smelled like lilac and lavender today. She would have to thank Ms. Amelia for freshening up the room before she'd arrived. Harbor snuggled into one of her pillows, closed her eyes, and savored the relaxing scent for a few calming breaths when she felt a thud hit the bed.

2

Harbor jolted. She held Theodore in a vice-like grip like he was a...weapon. It was not until she laid eyes on the intruder that she laid Theodore down, then quickly snatched him back up and began to pummel the trespasser.

Harbor's younger sister, Patrice, fought off the furry taps with a few playful shoves as she nearly choked in a fit of giggles.

"Okay, okay," Patrice begged. "I'm sorry. I give up."

Harbor held Theodore over Patrice's head like a weapon. She popped her sister over the head one last time and sat up. "I can't believe you scared me like that."

"That was too easy." She snatched Theodore from Harbor and cuddled the tuxedo-clad bear. "Glad you're home, Sis."

Slowly, painfully, Harbor said, "I'm glad I'm...."

Patrice threw up her hand. "Girl, please. Don't let that lie come out of your face. I know, Mama knows, everybody knows you do not want to be here."

Harbor ran a frustrated hand through her twist out. "Girl, thank you for keeping me honest."

Patrice sat up, holding Theodore to her chest. "As your baby sis, I take my job seriously." She gave Harbor a knowing grin. "You know I appreciate you, right?"

Harbor rested her chin on her knees. "I know," she responded, releasing a long, drawn-out sigh. "I'm assuming this is the part in the program where you tell me why you summoned me here and played your once-in-a-lifetime-anytime-any-place card."

Patrice stood, tossing Theodore to Harbor. She walked over to a large oak dresser with an attached mirror. Patrice studied her image. The woman staring back at her sported auburn spiral-curls with golden highlights that landed just above her shoulders. Patrice had fair skin like her mother, dotted with freckles and high cheekbones that Elizabeth swore were courtesy of Native American heritage in their family line.

She could neither confirm nor deny having Native American ancestry. If Patrice could ever get up her nerve to take one of those popular DNA tests, she might finally find out. Honestly, her big sister had always been the beauty of the family. Patrice looked at Harbor's reflection in the mirror and admired her sister's deep espresso complexion, full lips, and naturally thick eyelashes. She would not be surprised if Harbor was approached by a well-known toy company to design a doll in her likeness. Her big sis was just that cute.

Patrice bit down on her lower lip and chewed...a nervous habit she'd developed early in life. Acknowledging her expression was torn up, for lack of a better term, Patrice plastered on an all-is-well smile and turned to face Harbor.

"Sis, promise me you will make nice with Mama. All I want this week is a little cooperation."

Harbor eyed Patrice for a long moment. She stood and walked over to her baby sister, who was several inches taller but still a baby in her eyes. Harbor was about to pull big sis' rank.

"You and I both know that Mama and I do our best cooperating when there are several states between us," Harbor began. "So, what's really up, Treece? And don't take me on some long-drawn-out trip around the mulberry bush. Just say it."

Patrice shifted from one designer leather boot to the other. She crossed and then uncrossed her arms. Her next move found her pacing back and forth from the cozy picture window to the door, then back again. On Patrice's third cycle around the room, Harbor ran over and grabbed her sister's arm.

Harbor never thought of herself as violent, but at this point, she wanted to shake this news out of Patrice. A succession of three knocks on the bedroom door saved Harbor from some sort of shaken sister crime. Patrice seized the opportunity to escape Harbor's grasp and ran to the door.

Amelia stood on the other side, about to knock again. The discerning older woman looked from Harbor to Patrice, then back to Harbor. "You two are up to something," she stated as fact. "But since I know how to mind my own business, that's just what I plan on doing."

Patrice regained some of her confidence at the sight of her timely savior. She glanced at Harbor. "Just girl talk."

Harbor rolled her eyes.

"What's up, Ms. Amelia? Mama home?" Patrice asked, stepping just outside of the room.

Amelia took a small step out of her way. "I'm sure she'll be here soon enough with everybody else."

"Everybody else?" Harbor questioned. She eyed Patrice. "Who is everybody else, Treece?"

"Just people." Patrice grasped Amelia's hand and began to close the door. "And make sure you dress for dinner. The sneaks are cute but definitely not appropriate for tonight." She slammed the door.

Harbor stared daggers into her closed bedroom door. She had a feeling her mother wouldn't be the only emotional bridge she would cross this week.

***

When Harbor entered the dining room, she was the first of apparently several guests to arrive. Patrice had been ghost for the last several hours. *That girl always knew how to get lost and stay lost if she thought her sneaky little goose was about to get cooked*, Harbor thought.

She stood at the head of the table where her mother would take her place. On either side were four additional place settings. She and Patrice would claim two of the Queen Anne chairs. Who else was invited to this family dinner/reunion/whatever Patrice had in store meeting, Harbor wondered? And why the mystery?

Harbor plopped down in a chair furthest away from the head of the table. At that moment, Amelia walked in, carrying a set of flatware that sparkled as it caught the light from the chandelier.

Amelia frowned at Harbor and shooed her out of her newly claimed seat. "You will sit where you always sit, little missy." She replaced a set of flatware with the one she held. "To the right of your mama. Don't act like you don't know."

Harbor groaned. She rolled her neck from one side and then to the other. Her sad attempt at rolling away the stress was a complete bust. She could feel a migraine creeping its way behind her eyes. If she didn't shut this down now, she would never get through this evening that hadn't even started.

Harbor felt Amelia take hold of her hands. She knew before any words escaped those wise lips that Ms. Amelia was already praying for her. "God, I just want to say thank you for bringing our Harbor home to us. You know exactly what our baby girl needs."

Harbor felt the tears beginning to flow, and the tension release its hold. She held onto Amelia's hands and her petition to God for dear life.

"Yes, God, arm her with strength for this battle. Thank you, Lord. Amen." Amelia ended the prayer and leaned down to kiss Harbor's cheek sweetly.

Harbor opened her eyes, now filled with tears. "You always know," she said, barely able to speak. She couldn't get into the whole "strength for the battle" piece. She wasn't ready to be in the ring for no kind of battle.

Amelia smiled. "He always knows. I just try to keep these ears tuned in to what He got to say."

Harbor thanked God someone kept their ears open to what He had to say. She looked again at the number of place settings. "Are you eating with us tonight?"

"No, ma'am. I got church business this evening. Then I got dinner plans with Deacon Bradley."

"Excuse me," Harbor cooed. "Who is Deacon Bradley?"

Amelia looked directly at Harbor. "My business." She snickered, walking out of the dining room.

Harbor shook her head. She dabbed at the moisture beneath her eyes. The doorbell rang as she sucked in a cleansing sniffle to avoid blowing her nose.

Harbor heard Patrice's favorite Mary Jane's racing down the stairs to greet whoever was on the other side of the door. Elizabeth had not made her grand entrance, for which Harbor was grateful. She needed a minute to literally fix her face.

Harbor picked up a knife and peered at her reflection. *Great.* The twenty minutes she'd spent trying to do something with her makeup was a bust. She picked up her emerald, green napkin and dabbed at the remaining moisture on her cheeks.

Get it together, Girl, she chided herself.

Harbor had no idea why she had broken down at Ms. Amelia's prayer. Ms. Amelia had always prayed for her or anyone else that needed a little Jesus. She never asked for permission. No, the older woman just let the Holy Spirit use her. That's just who she was, and Harbor loved her for it. She could always count on Ms. Amelia to keep her lifted up in prayer, which she absolutely needed, especially today.

Harbor stood, smoothing imagined wrinkles from her little black dress with the ruffled V-neck and ruffled white sash. She walked to her seat, positioned just to the right of Elizabeth. Even when her father was alive, Elizabeth sat at the head of the table with her husband to her left and eldest daughter to her right. That's the way it had always been. *And that is the way it shall remain.*

Harbor could hear laughter coming from the foyer and the distinctive click of Patrice's heels headed toward the dining room. She inhaled one good cleansing breath and then released.

All the inhaling and exhaling in the name of yoga could not have prepared Harbor for what she saw walking into her space. It was a good thing she stood behind her seat with her hands firmly attached to the chair because her right leg started doing that uncontrollable shake thing it did when her nerves decided to run the show.

Harbor watched as Patrice glided into the room, wearing a smile as wide as Texas and a glow that could have lit up the state all on its own. Soft curls framed her petite face, and the couture turquoise dress she wore made her look youthful and like a woman in charge all at the same time.

The man whose arm Patrice laid claim to was not a new face to Harbor. Colin Banks had captured Patrice's heart during their junior year as co-captains of the Tanner High Debate Team. Colin was a good guy and loved her sister wholeheartedly. It didn't hurt that Colin was easy on the eyes with looks to rival a box-office movie hero. His light-brown complexion always seemed to glow when he was in Patrice's presence. For that, Harbor was truly thankful.

Now, the man escorting her mother into the dining room was another matter entirely. Why was Ahmad Ferebee, the man formerly known as her fiancé, in her space, accompanying *her* mother into the room like he owned the place? Harbor's steely gaze darted from Patrice to Ahmad, then landed on her mother.

Harbor glared at her mother, who looked like a seasoned version of Patrice with fair skin and chin-length, auburn tresses. Elizabeth gave her a half smile, half smirk. Harbor offered her mother a suspicious, raised eyebrow in return.

Elizabeth allowed Ahmad to walk her to the head of the table. Ahmad pulled out Elizabeth's chair and gave it the slightest push forward as she took her seat.

Elizabeth rested her hand on his. "You were always such a gentleman, Ahmad."

What is this? Harbor wanted to scream. Instead, she coughed and nearly strangled herself with her own saliva, trying to avoid saying every jacked-up thing that came to her mind.

Ahmad rushed to her side. She shooed him away.

"Girl, you okay?" Patrice asked as Colin pulled out her chair.

Harbor took a few long sips of water. "Peachy." She wanted the response to sound terse, but it sounded more like a decade's old smoker's cough.

She looked back at Ahmad, who was standing at her side, waiting for what exactly...a special invitation to park his six-foot self in a chair like everybody else?

Harbor decided to let him off the hook...this time. "I'm fine."

Ahmad smiled that beautifully wide grin that used to make Harbor feel all kinds of special. Now, she just wanted to slap that goofy grin off his face.

"Well, good," Ahmad responded, seeming totally unfazed by Harbor's attempt at nonchalance. "I'd hate to think my presence caused *you* distress after all these years."

The hint of sarcasm in Ahmad's voice hit Harbor in the gut. She guessed breaking off their engagement without an explanation and essentially cutting off all communication could make a person feel salty. She would allow him that much. However, Harbor had no intentions of playing the what-really-happened-to-us-five-years-ago game with Ahmad. It's simple, really. They were engaged. She broke it off. They moved on with their separate lives. End of story.

Harbor was about to tell Ahmad as much when she felt the soft, manicured touch of her mother's hand barely brush her hand.

"It's so nice to have you home, Harbor."

Well, the surprises just keep coming.

Never at a loss for words, Harbor could not get her brain to form a response. So, she just stared at the woman who'd told her if she left home, she should stay gone. That's what she should have done...stayed gone, Harbor realized. Tiptoeing across these emotional minefields was for the birds.

She slowly slid her hand from beneath Elizabeth's grasp and laid it on her lap. Harbor swallowed hard and blinked, trying to regain her composure after feeling like she'd gotten hit with a brick.

Patrice caught Harbor's gaze. Her baby sis smiled in that special way, letting Harbor know she was not alone.

In what was probably too peppy of a voice for the awkward moment, Patrice said, "We're all glad Harbor is home." The sisters, who were always tight, locked gazes, adding another thread to their forever got-your-back quilt. "And at just the right time."

Harbor narrowed her eyes. "For?"

Patrice looked away. Her gaze shifted between looking at the moon glistening off the lake just beyond the large bay window to an imaginary water stain on her fork. Her vibrant almond-shaped eyes found interest in looking at anything and everything but Harbor.

"Harbor, it's like this," Colin began as he and Patrice intertwined their fingers. "Patrice and I...."

Patrice shook her head so vigorously it looked like her perfectly spiraled curls would hop off her head and roll down the center of the table. Colin raised her chin with his index finger so that their eyes met. At his touch, Patrice's anxiety seemed to instantly vanish.

"I love your sister more than anything on this earth," Colin spoke to Harbor, but his eyes never shifted, even a moment, from Patrice's loving gaze. "Your amazing sister has agreed to become my wife this Saturday."

Harbor coughed, and she thought she might actually choke. This time, she didn't bother with the water. She needed some answers.

"You mean like six days from today, Saturday?"

When Patrice finally found her voice, she said, "It's actually six days, two hours and three minutes."

"But who's counting," Patrice and Colin cooed in unison.

Harbor and Ahmad uttered a collective, "Wow."

Patrice reached across the table for Elizabeth and Harbor's hands. Both complied. Almost whispering, Patrice said, "I always thought Daddy would walk me down the aisle, guiding me to my happily ever after." Her eyes glistened with unshed tears. "But Daddy is gone. So, on Saturday, I want my one and only Mama and my one and only big sis to walk me down the aisle."

3

The migraine Ms. Amelia helped to keep at bay with her prayers and supplications to God on Harbor's behalf came back with a vengeance just after Patrice's request for a mother and sister duo to walk her down the aisle. Harbor had attempted to make nice for a full fifteen minutes. She busied herself, trying not to make eye-contact with her mother or Ahmad while they oohed and aahed over Patrice and Colin's super stupid let's-get-married-in-six-days wedding announcement.

The moment her migraine moved from a possibility to the point of no return, Harbor gave her apologies and headed upstairs to her room. She loved her sister more than anything or anyone, but this was extra even for Patrice.

The almost imperceptible knock on Harbor's bedroom door came soon after she'd pulled her disappearing act. Her first inclination was to ignore the would-be intruder. Whatever emotional energy Harbor had stored up for this week of surprises was already depleted. And it was only day one, she groaned.

Another tap.

Harbor decided it must be Patrice coming to beg her pardon. She had a mind to make her sweat it out, but even that would take more energy than she was willing to give.

When Harbor opened the door, she reached to yank Patrice into the room for a sisterly come to Jesus but stopped short when she saw her mother's piercing hazel eyes staring back at her. At that moment,

Harbor's already muddled brain decided to take an unsolicited trip back to the last time mother and daughter were face-to-face at the threshold of her bedroom door.

It was the morning of her father's funeral. It was the morning Harbor knew living in her childhood home without the man she affectionately called "Buff" was no longer an option. Her buffer was gone. The welcomed bit of cushion and calmness Bradford Wilson became every time Harbor and Elizabeth were in breathing distance of each other was gone.

Dressed in a magnolia-white pantsuit to honor the bright, shining light her father gave to the world for nearly sixty-four years, Harbor had felt something like peace wash over and envelop her as she prepared to say goodbye to her father. At that moment, she'd felt the familiar warmth of her father's embrace. That sense of "all is well" washed away like a tidal wave with a head-to-toe perusal from Elizabeth that screamed she was not impressed with Harbor's celebratory ensemble.

Dressed in a sleek, black pantsuit, Elizabeth looked like a grieving widow but sounded like a tyrant.

"You will not leave this house wearing that." Harbor remembered Elizabeth's command like it was yesterday instead of a lifetime ago. "Change," she'd demanded.

Harbor couldn't say if it was the reality of burying her father or of turning twenty-one on the very same day that sent her over the edge, but she had had enough. Whatever *it* was, it was coming Elizabeth's way.

Harbor walked past her mother toward the stairs and turned. "I'm not changing," she'd said with more confidence than she'd felt. Thank God for wide pants legs because her legs embarked on their own nervous dance party no one with good sense would accept an invitation to. "I'm going to the church to say goodbye to Daddy. He wouldn't want me to change, so I'm not going to. Then, I'm going to find myself a cupcake because it's my birthday."

Harbor hadn't given Elizabeth the option of responding. She'd raced down the stairs and into a waiting family car. After all of the "goodbyes" had been said and the last hymn was sung over her father's gold-trimmed casket, Harbor walked out of the church into a taxi. Destination unknown. The one thing Harbor did know with certainty...137 Briarfield Lane was no longer her home. She hadn't even returned to the house to pack her things.

Five years later, she stood in front of a woman she would never understand. *This is awkward*, Harbor acknowledged. She stepped aside, allowing Elizabeth to enter.

Back erect and head held high, Elizabeth tentatively stepped into Harbor's space.

Yeah, this is awkward, Harbor confirmed as she continued to stand by the door. The open door was her only option if she wanted to quickly exit if this little reunion went south.

"Amelia...well, I thought you might need these," Elizabeth said as she handed Harbor a bottle of pain reliever.

Harbor accepted the bottle of six-to-eight-hour relief with some hesitation, then checked herself with a mental shake. Regardless of the status of her relationship with Elizabeth, the pills weren't poisonous.

"Thank you," Harbor finally said.

Elizabeth nodded. "I see you changed your hair," Elizabeth's words came out like a sad attempt at small talk, which it was.

Harbor self-consciously ran her fingers through her twist out that was a little less twist and a lot more out than she would have preferred after much too long of a day. She folded her arms across her chest. "It's been five years," she responded coolly. Her gaze was fixed on Elizabeth, who almost looked...uncomfortable, which did not fit the self-assured persona of her mother. "A lot has changed."

"I would imagine so," Elizabeth responded after a few uncomfortable moments. She walked toward Harbor and stopped. "Take the pills before too long. It's best to get a hold of a migraine early before it turns into something else entirely." With that, Elizabeth made her way out of Harbor's room and shut the door.

When the door closed, Harbor slid to the floor, eyeing the bottle of pain reliever. Her frilly black dress was picking up all kinds of lint from the beige carpet, but that was the least of her concern. The knock-down, drag-out she'd expected to get into with Elizabeth turned into a masterclass in the anticlimactic.

"What kind of high-level foolishness is this?" She wondered aloud. Patrice had some explaining to do.

***

The next morning, Harbor popped out of bed like a splash of water hitting a heated cast iron skillet. She needed answers, and the only person who knew all the dirt, so to speak, was Patrice.

She grabbed her robe from the foot of her bed and slid her arms through the smooth silk fibers. The elegant but thin rose gold garment did little to alleviate the morning chill that settled over her room. Still, it would have to do, Harbor decided. Cold air to her bare flesh always felt like an assault, especially in the morning. Today wasn't any different. But she didn't have an extra second to mull over making her dreams of cozy warmth a priority.

Harbor tossed on the socks she'd kicked off sometime during the night and tiptoed over to her door. She pressed her ear against the door, knowing the distinct sound of her target would enter the hallway in five, four, three, two.

Harbor threw the door open. She watched her sister hop and pop down the hallway singing *Love on Top* in a version that gave the term tone-deaf its definition. When Patrice reached her door, Harbor dragged her into the room and slammed the door. She grabbed Patrice's arm, pulled her toward the bed, and not so gently forced her to take a seat.

Desperate times.

"Girl, what is wrong with you?" Patrice asked. "You know I need my solitary, singing time before I start my day. I don't do early morning drama," she warned with a raised finger.

Harbor stood in front of her with arms folded across her chest. She tapped her foot methodically like she was gearing up to tap dance across a stage. The sigh that escaped her lips could not be contained even if she had wanted it to.

"Patrice. Girl. You." Forming a coherent sentence became an impossible task. "Ooh," she screamed, throwing up her hands.

Wide-eyed, Patrice slid a little further into the comfort and safety of the bed. She spotted Theodore snuggling beneath the plush quilt and picked him up. She waved him back and forth like a fluffy flag of surrender.

"Truce," she begged.

Harbor cast her baby sister a long-suffering glare, then made her way to the bed. She snatched Theodore and flopped against her pillows. "Start talking," she demanded.

Patrice groaned and bit her lower lip. She drew her knees to her chin and cradled herself for a moment, then said, "So, it kind of sort of started like," she rambled.

Harbor cut her off. "No, we are not doing the "What had happened" game. You need to start with this wedding countdown, then make a pit stop with what's going on with Mama. Then slide your way into explaining why I was in the same space with my ex-fiancé, Ahmad, last night."

Patrice threw up her hands in surrender. "Okay, okay. I know this is...a lot," she finally said. "So, the wedding is easy. I love Colin, and he loves me. It's that simple."

Harbor rolled her eyes. "If it was that simple, why didn't you tell me before last night? And why the rush? Why not six months from now or a year?

Patrice pointed an accusing finger at her sister. "That's why. You would have given me every reason to wait and wait and wait until I was five days away from drawing my first Social Security payment." Patrice laughed, and Harbor joined in. "You know it's true."

Harbor sobered. "You're right. I'm not in a rush for my baby sister to get married." She reached over to hug Patrice. She released Patrice and looked into her eyes. "I'm happy for you, Sis. You deserve all the good."

Patrice smiled and did a little happy dance. "I do. Don't I?" She giggled, then sighed. "And so do you."

Harbor clutched Theodore to her chest. She knew processing her happiness was not up for discussion, so she not so stealthily changed the subject. "Okay, so I accept this beeline for the altar explanation," she began with a raised brow. "But I need a bit more detail about why my lioness of a mama is acting like a baby lamb."

Patrice huffed. "A baby lamb...please. Elizabeth Wilson is nobody's lamb," Patrice began slowly. She was trying to figure out exactly how to describe the transformation that occurred with her mother after her father's death. Patrice moved from the foot of the bed to sit beside Harbor. "After Daddy died and you left, Mama was a mess. She stayed in her room for almost two weeks. Ms. Amelia and I tried everything, but nothing we said or did made a difference."

Harbor's eyes grew wide. She couldn't imagine her take-it-by-force mother giving into even great grief. She shook her head. "That's just crazy. Why didn't you tell me?"

"Would you have come home?" Patrice asked in her zero-pretense way.

Harbor sighed and answered honestly. "No."

"Exactly," Patrice responded. "So, I didn't bother telling you. We just gave her time to do whatever she needed to do and prayed. Ms. Amelia and I did a lot of praying." She looped her hand through the crook of her sister's arm.

Harbor felt a pang of guilt, knowing her mother had suffered, in what seemed like the worst way, after her father's death. She and Elizabeth were never on the same page about almost anything. It was just the nature of their relationship, and she had come to accept that as just life. But if her mother's pain mirrored even a tenth of what Harbor felt after her father's death, the grief certainly chipped away at a bit of her spirit that would never return.

Harbor gently squeezed Patrice's hand. "I get Mama going into deep grief after Daddy died," she began slowly. "But this whole mellow mama routine and bringing me pain reliever for a migraine version is just weird."

Patrice laughed so hard she nearly choked. "Girl, you are so dramatic," she cleared her throat, then said, "Look, I don't honestly know what happened with Mama. I just know *it* happened."

Harbor nodded. She still did not understand but had no idea what else to do. "So, what's next?" She asked.

Patrice hopped from the bed and darted to the door. "Breakfast with Mama," she said, gripping the doorknob.

"Excuse me," Harbor interjected, rolling her neck from one side and then to the other. "Breakfast?"

"Yes, in twenty," Patrice spouted off quickly. She maneuvered one foot out the door. "And lunch with Ahmad at noon."

Before Harbor could jump off the bed and chase Patrice down, the door was already slammed shut. She heard her sister scampering down the stairs and decided not to give chase. Harbor knew her strengths, and running did not rank among them. She soothed herself with the knowledge that at some point in the next five days, she and Patrice would be alone again. When that happened, her baby sis would get a lot more than a piece of her mind, which Harbor was losing with each passing moment.

4

Harbor walked into the kitchen with precisely two minutes to spare. The fragrance of spiced French toast, maple sausage links, and parmesan scrambled eggs enveloped her. *This is heaven.* Wait, why was she smelling a playlist of her all-time favorite breakfast items?

Harbor chided herself with a mental shake. *Stop being a weirdo.* This delightful breakfast menu must be Ms. Amelia's way of welcoming her home properly. However, when Harbor spied Ms. Amelia at the stove and leaned in to offer her a thank-you hug, she knew this little welcome-home breakfast resembled something closer to a delightfully delicious bribe. A bribe she was willing to accept...for now.

Ms. Amelia added the last few sausage links to the platter. Harbor attempted to snag one of the links, but Ms. Amelia's quick trigger hand popped her before she could even get close.

"You ain't been gone that long," Ms. Amelia warned. She covered the platter with a top and placed it on the island beside a container of orange juice and a jar of maple syrup. Ms. Amelia pointed to the juice and syrup. "Take those outside. I'll be right behind you."

Harbor did as requested. "Why are we eating outside? Mom hates bugs."

Their mutual hatred of all God's special, little crawly creatures was one point Harbor could agree wholeheartedly with Elizabeth.

Fighting gnats and flies while trying to enjoy a meal, even one prepared by Ms. Amelia, made no sense.

Amelia picked up the platter and two sets of utensils and headed for the sliding door. When Amelia walked up to the door, she stepped aside and waited for Harbor to open the door.

"Is eating breakfast on your mind this morning or asking me a million questions?"

With the orange juice tucked under her arm and the syrup in her left hand, Harbor reached for the door. Before she could call Ms. Amelia out on whatever was going on, the door slid open.

Harbor looked up to see Ahmad looking as fine and unwelcome as he wanted to be, grinning at her like he was her guest. She glanced from Ahmad to Ms. Amelia. Harbor was not surprised Ms. Amelia had maneuvered her slender frame past Ahmad and made a beeline for the patio set.

"This food's getting cold," Ms. Amelia yelled over her shoulder. "Y'all get a move on."

Harbor groaned. She didn't know how long she'd stood there, staring daggers at Ms. Amelia's back. By the time she remembered Ahmad was still there, he gawked at her like she needed more help than he could provide.

No, she did not need a psychological intervention. She needed answers.

Ahmad reached for the orange juice. "You good?"

Ignoring his question, Harbor maneuvered her way out the door and past Ahmad, just as Ms. Amelia had done minutes before. When she reached the table, she was not surprised that Ms. "Too Sneaky for Her Own Good" Amelia had made a speedy exit.

Harbor placed the syrup on the patio table, which had two, not three, place settings. Math was never her thing, but even she realized Elizabeth would not make an appearance for whatever this was.

Wait, what is this? Harbor wondered as she plopped down in the incredibly soft, cushioned seat. As much as she wanted to feel some kind of way, the coziness of her chair felt like luxuriating at a five-star resort. Harbor would never complain about Elizabeth's taste in the finer things.

She leaned into the chair, closing her eyes, completely aware she was "neglecting her hostess duties," as Elizabeth would say. Harbor heard, rather than saw, Ahmad placing the orange juice on the table and taking the lid off the platter. The savory aroma almost gave her the incentive to ignore her unwanted guest and fill her plate and her tummy.

Ahmad began to fill his plate. "So, you plan on sitting there, letting Ms. Amelia's breakfast get cold?" He asked through a mouthful of food.

Harbor's eyes flew open. She sat up straight, grabbing a sausage link from the platter and savoring one delectable bite of maple goodness then another before she asked, "Why are you here?"

Ahmad took a sip of his orange juice. He hunched his broad shoulders. "Elizabeth sent me a text this morning. She said she had something to take care of and couldn't make breakfast with you. Asked me if I could take her place." He smiled. "So, you get me."

No offense to Ahmad, but really? *She* had something better to do, Harbor inwardly complained. *Don't let a little thing like your firstborn coming home for the first time in five years get in the way of your plans.*

Harbor stabbed her fork with a few of the fluffy parmesan eggs. She savored the taste. Right or wrong, a forkful of good food had a way of setting her funky attitude to rights. *Thank you, Ms. Amelia.*

Ahmad pointed to Harbor's empty plate. "You know you can put your food on that empty round thing. It makes eating a lot easier."

Ahmad picked up the plate and filled it with all of Harbor's favorite breakfast treats.

Harbor waved a hand. "You don't have to do that. I'm a big girl. I can make my own plate."

Ahmad added extra sausage links to the plate and placed it in front of Harbor.

Harbor poured an excessive amount of maple syrup on her French toast. "Thank you."

Ahmad's eyes widened with each long pour of syrup. The stream of sugary goodness resembled a floating caramel river. "I had forgotten how real your sweet tooth is," he said, sliding the syrup to the other side of the table. "You need to slow down before you start running around here like a five-year-old on Halloween."

Don't laugh, Harbor admonished herself two seconds before she broke out in a fit of giggles. She hit Ahmad's shoulder. "Shut up." Harbor did not want to love being in Ahmad's company again. She did not want to love that it felt like they were picking up where they left off. Well, not exactly where they left off, Harbor thought. Maybe it felt like they were picking up one or two steps before everything went horribly wrong.

Harbor took another bite of French toast and placed her fork on her plate. She glanced at Ahmad. He stared at the glistening lake just beyond the patio like it harbored every answer he would ever need.

"Why would my mother put you in as her substitute for breakfast?" Harbor asked. "I've eaten breakfast every day by myself for the last five years. It's nothing new."

At this admission, Ahmad gave Harbor his full attention. Whatever spell the lake had cast over him vanished on the heels of the next breeze. "That is literally the saddest thing I have ever heard," Ahmad responded. He put his pointer finger up to his temple as if he was in deep thought. "Nope, I cannot think of anything sadder than that."

Harbor took a sip of her juice and waved a dismissive hand. "It's just breakfast. It's not that serious," she said, but the admission sounded lame to her ears. Of course, it was pathetic she had not eaten breakfast or many other meals with anyone except herself in a very long time. *Leave it to Ahmad to put a spotlight on my sad social existence,* she thought.

"Hey," Ahmad said, summoning Harbor's attention. "Did Colin or Patrice let you know I would be at dinner last night? Or was that an engagement party? I don't know." He laughed.

"Not a word," Harbor responded. She looked Ahmad in the eyes before she asked, "What about you?"

"Ha!" He threw his head back, making his locs sway from side to side. "Not a peep."

"Rude."

"Exactly."

Harbor pushed her plate aside.

Ahmad looked at Harbor's nearly empty plate and stood. He offered his hand.

Harbor stared at Ahmad's hand for a second too long. *Don't make this even more uncomfortable than it already is*, Harbor warned herself. She placed her hand in his and stood. "Where are we off to?" Harbor asked, knowing she would accompany Ahmad wherever he wanted to go.

Ahmad pushed his chair to the table. "You and I have an appointment to meet your mom at Kelsey's Guys & Gals to find something fancy for this wedding," he crooned.

Harbor cocked her head. Okay, her attitude was back and ready to feast. "Should I be offended that you are privy to these little wedding details?" She asked, daring him not to take this seriously. "This is my family, and yet I'm kind of on the outside looking in at this thing. That ain't right."

Harbor cut off her mini tirade and shifted her gaze toward the lake, seeming to search for the same answers Ahmad had searched for moments earlier. The shimmering sun reflecting off the water gave Harbor a momentary sense of peace. She needed to find a way to string together more than a moment or two of peace because this emotional bouncy house foolishness had to stop.

Ahmad followed Harbor's gaze toward the lake. "We could skip out on the whole clothes-buying thing and hang out here the way we used to," he offered, nudging her shoulder. "I'm like sixty-nine percent sure Patrice and Colin won't mind if we show up on their big day wearing jeans and matching tees." Ahmad took a quick peek at Harbor's footwear. "And red sneaks."

Harbor laughed and nudged him back. It felt right to be in Ahmad's presence again. It felt right that they had fallen right back in step. No, she would not overanalyze why her five-year hiatus away from Mr. Ahmad Ferebee felt like nothing more than a day. A day! A thorough and complete daytime tv analysis of her wonky love life could take place on her flight back to Atlanta at the end of the week. But not today.

Harbor grabbed another sausage link from the platter. "Patrice and Colin only have eyes for each other." Harbor laughed. "We could show up in matching clown suits and polka dot berets, and those two wouldn't blink. Now, Elizabeth Wilson, that's a whole other story." She began walking back toward the house.

Ahmad nodded and ran to catch up, knowing Harbor's mother would give them both a dignified tongue-lashing if they did not look the part of a well-dressed best man and maid of honor. As cool as Ms. Elizabeth acted when he was around, Ahmad had heard enough stories throughout the years to know he did not want to find himself on her wrong side. That distinction seemed strictly set aside for Harbor, which he hated to admit.

Even while they'd dated in high school and throughout their abbreviated engagement, just before her father passed, mother and daughter were constantly at odds. From her wardrobe to her hairstyle to the college she chose, Harbor's decision-making skills were always up for debate. Ahmad could not imagine butting heads with his mother over every little thing. Being a silent witness to Harbor and Elizabeth's relationship was exhausting. Still, he would have gladly stayed the course till death do them part if Harbor had given him a chance to.

Harbor tossed the remaining sausage in her mouth and opened the sliding door. "Let me grab my purse, and I'll meet you out front," Harbor said as she stepped into the kitchen. She noticed Ms. Amelia was nowhere in sight. *No worries*, Harbor thought. *I will catch up with Little Ms. Match Maker at some point.*

Ahmad walked with Harbor through the living room to the front door. She took the stairs two at a time before turning around when she reached the top. "Give me five minutes, and I'm all yours," Harbor said, nearly out of breath before disappearing into her bedroom.

"I'm all yours, too," Ahmad murmured on his way out the front door. "If only you'd let me."

***

When Ahmad pulled up to Kelsey's Guys and Gals twenty minutes ago, he'd assumed he and Harbor would have made their way into the chic boutique, found appropriate wedding ware, and made their way back to the house before the lunch crowd emerged from the office buildings in downtown Norfolk. He was wrong.

As soon as he pulled up to the newest store to offer "dress clothes," as his mama would say, Harbor shut down. Her ability to form a coherent sentence...gone. And he had a feeling her presence in his passenger seat constituted legal residence. While Ahmad could get with being in Harbor's company for any reason or no reason at all, this whole thing bordered on odd...even for Harbor. He needed to try another approach besides saying her name on repeat.

Ahmad placed a gentle hand on Harbor's arm. "I'll tell you a secret. Kelsey Chance, the owner of this fine establishment, is my first cousin," he confided. "I promise you, she's good people and does not bite. Except when I pulled at her braids in the third grade, but that is a really long story. And I probably deserved it."

If Ahmad hoped to get a laugh out of Harbor or even a bit of recognition, he was pathetically mistaken. The woman did not utter a word. Instead, Harbor continued to stare at the shop like she would rather eat rocks than step one foot inside the single-story boutique.

Ahmad removed his hand from her arm and reached for her chin. Slowly, he turned her head, so their eyes met. "Tink, what's up?" Ahmad realized if the nickname he'd given Harbor a million years ago when they were each other's everything did not jolt her out of this trance, nothing would.

The long-a-go-name that only meant something to them had its intended effect. Harbor sighed and stared at Ahmad for a long moment, which should have been several steps beyond uncomfortable, but it wasn't. Ahmad Ferebee personified patience. If possible, he was even more patient than Stanley, her rideshare driver.

Oh Lord, am I really holding another man hostage in his own car? Harbor groaned. Running into her mother, even on a planned excursion, messed with her policy of being emotionally detached from all things concerning Elizabeth. She had to get it together, or this week would cause permanent mental distress.

She simultaneously unbuckled her seat belt and broke their gazes. Staring into those milk chocolate eyes would be her undoing. So, like a big girl, Harbor opened her door and hopped out of the vehicle like all was well. She started to walk toward the shop, then turned around to yell back at Ahmad, "You coming?"

Ahmad reached across the seat for the passenger door handle. Before he yanked the door closed that Harbor "forgot" to close, he yelled back, "Woman, we are going to talk."

Harbor offered Ahmad her sweetest smile and rushed into the boutique. She had no intentions of taking a deep dive into her relationship with her mother, especially with Ahmad.

Ahmad Ferebee, a man who served as the unofficial psychologist of their small group of friends back in the day, had a way of getting down to the truth of a thing without pretense and without flourish. Why Harbor did not see this come to Jesus with Ahmad concerning Elizabeth, she did not know. Even after a five-year absence with literally zero communication, Ahmad could still swoop in and talk her into being emotionally available.

"That ain't happening," Harbor blurted out before she could stop herself.

If the stylishly dressed woman wearing a form-fitting maxi dress and wedge sandals had seen Harbor playing the crazy lady role, she did not show it. Before Harbor could object or throw up the time-out sign, the woman with smooth caramel skin and flowing ebony curls cascading down her back enveloped her in a hug. It had been a minute since Harbor had been in Virginia, but she couldn't remember when it was all good for strangers to act so touchy-feely.

After a moment, the woman stepped back, held Harbor at arm's length, and smiled, showing off her pearly whites.

Harbor smiled in return because what else was she supposed to do? Nothing she did could possibly make this encounter any more awkward. Smiles made everything better, right?

"I am so excited to finally meet you, Love," the woman sang.

Ah, the puzzle pieces in Harbor's muddled brain began to come together. This woman, this over-exuberant, over-excitable woman, was Ahmad's cousin, Kelsey. She should have known. Joyful optimism must run deep in the Ferebee line.

"Kelsey!" Ahmad proclaimed when he walked into the shop.

As soon as Ahmad entered the shop, Harbor decided this was her best and likely only opportunity to escape out of Ms. Kelsey's grasp. She watched with awe as the cousins embraced each other with a hug that screamed: "Family Forever." If Harbor did not know any better, she would think Kelsey and Ahmad had not seen each other in a very long time. Ahmad confirmed her suspicions with his next words.

"I missed you, Kels," Ahmad said when he finally released Kelsey from their hug. "It's been too long."

Kelsey playfully tapped Ahmad's shoulder. "You do get how travel works," she responded. "Charlotte is just a hop, skip, and...."

Ahmad took a playful jump toward his cousin. "And a jump away. I know. I know." He enveloped her in another embrace. "But I'm glad you decided to open a store downtown. We need your good vibes."

Kelsey spun around with arms opened wide. "Always good vibes. Only good vibes. Ooh, that should have been my tagline." Kelsey laughed with a joy that bordered on infectious. Ahmad joined in.

Harbor stood near the door, watching this heartwarming scene of familial love play out. As close as Kelsey and Ahmad seemed, she wondered why her former fiancé had neglected to tell her about a relationship that was obviously very important to him. Harbor had always believed she and Ahmad shared everything. Well, maybe not everything.

Ahmad had proudly claimed the title of "Mr. Open Book" when they were together. That man wore his feelings on his sleeve like a badge of honor. On the other hand, Harbor was the book with several redacted pages and maybe a few missing chapters. Could she blame him for not wanting to bare his soul? *Absolutely.*

Before Harbor could work herself into feeling some kind of way about Ahmad's willful omission, she found his hand around her waist, pulling her into this little family reunion. His touch felt good and so right. It felt like the best parts of their past and a whisper of what the future could be.

If Harbor thought she had gotten over Ahmad in the years they had been apart, the only person she was fooling was herself. Ahmad was not a man that one just got over by sheer will and fortitude. Lord knows Harbor tried her best to feel nothing for this man. As she slid more into his embrace, Harbor knew she'd already failed the keep-Ahmad-at-least-six-feet-away test. Where were her handy-dandy Covid protocols when she needed them? Harbor sent up a silent prayer God would guard her heart against falling more deeply than she already had.

Ahmad was a good man. He was the kind of man that would trip over himself to avoid stepping on an ant. Harbor had witnessed this man almost cause himself bodily harm to avoid trampling those annoying little insects that made her skin crawl. But Ahmad had respect for all things great and small, which was one of the reasons she had fallen in love with him. Was he perfect? No. Was Ahmad a once-in-a-lifetime opportunity? Yes! So why couldn't Harbor get her stuff together and fall back into his arms? She had no idea.

While Harbor could appreciate the playful banter between cousins, they had business to attend to. If she stayed focused, she could meet all her obligations for this lightning-fast wedding and avoid falling back into old patterns with Ahmad. Then she'd hop on a plane back to Atlanta and back to her life, which was starting to feel a little sad and pathetically lonely.

Note to self, when you get home, find a life.

"So, Kelsey," Harbor began, not so stealthily inserting herself into their conversation. "Ahmad and I are meeting my mother, Elizabeth, to find outfits for my sister's wedding this Saturday."

Kelsey giggled and threw her hands up like she was swatting flies at a church picnic. "Oh, my word. Ahmad and I are just going on and on. Charge it to my head, Honey, not my heart." She spun on her chunky heels and dashed for the front counter. She grabbed an envelope and returned to them in a flash. Kelsey handed the envelope to Harbor like she'd just found a winning lottery ticket. "Ms. Elizabeth asked me to give this to you."

Harbor stared at the envelope. Why would Elizabeth have shown up well before they were scheduled to meet and written Harbor a note? Although she felt anxious about playing nice with her mother today, Harbor didn't know how to feel about not seeing her at all. Was Elizabeth avoiding her? Did Harbor just get ghosted by the woman that gave birth to her? *That ain't right.*

Harbor took the envelope. "Thank you." She tucked the envelope under her arm. Harbor almost did not recognize the transition of Ahmad's hand from her waist to her hand. She looked at their intertwined fingers and was a second, maybe two, from breaking out into an ugly cry.

"Give us a second, Kels," Ahmad said, offering his cousin a conciliatory wink.

"You got it," Kelsey responded. She smiled at Harbor. "Take your time, Honey. I'll be around if y'all need me. And trust me, whatever you choose, you will look amazing. It's hard to improve on perfection." Kelsey turned to leave. If possible, the young woman had even more pep in her step as she greeted a new customer.

Ahmad turned to Harbor, giving her hand a little squeeze. "You okay, Tink?"

"Nope." At that moment, the tears began to fall. Crying in public was not Harbor's thing, but this well of emotions had a really determined, really forceful mind of its own. She recognized, more than felt, Ahmad draw her into his arms. She prayed God would turn this spigot off, but He seemed to have other plans.

Harbor couldn't gauge how long the tears continued to blaze a freefall down her cheeks *or* how she and Ahmad ended up sitting on a cozy little bench at the back of the store.

This is crazy. Harbor wanted to scream. She hadn't even read Elizabeth's note *and* was still a mess.

Harbor hesitantly removed her head from the comfort of Ahmad's chest. "I'm sorry," she said in a voice that resembled an unwelcome aftershock after an earthquake.

"For what?" Ahmad asked and raised Harbor's chin so that their eyes met. "Don't apologize for feeling."

Harbor wiped her eyes. She sat up straight, creating space between herself and this beautiful man. She held up the envelope. Slowly, Harbor pulled the single sheet from its confinement.

Harbor read the note aloud.

'Harbor, my apologies for not being able to meet with you and Ahmad today. Something came up. I've already picked out my outfit and asked Kelsey to pull a few that would work well for you. Please give Ahmad my apologies as well. Best, Mom.'

Harbor tucked the letter and envelope in her purse.

Ahmad stood. He offered Harbor his hand. She placed her hand in his and stood. "Let's get out of here."

"After all this drama, I can't leave here without something to wear," she said, shaking her head as if the motion would set her to rights. "No, we will find an appropriate outfit for this wedding and hopefully convince your cousin I am not a complete whack job."

At those words, Ahmad threw his head back in laughter. His well-groomed locs that hit just above his shoulders shook back and forth. "Kelsey is the last one to call anybody whacky. When we were twelve, Kelsey stopped traffic walking home from school one day to practice a dance move that just "came to her." Said she didn't want to lose the vibe. Whatever that means. I love my cuz, but she is slightly to the left of crazy."

Harbor laughed. "Yeah, that's a bit much," she acknowledged. Harbor looked across the store and nodded toward Kelsey, who was helping a hopelessly lost woman coordinate an outfit. "But she's sweet. Why didn't you ever tell me about her?"

Ahmad hunched his shoulders. "Never came up, I guess," he responded, walking toward the front of the store.

Harbor watched Ahmad for a moment as he walked up to Kelsey. He leaned down to give his cousin a hug. *I'm not the only secret keeper, Mr. Ahmad*, Harbor thought. *Never came up.* She wiped the remaining tears from her eyes, fixed her face as best she could, and walked to the front of the store.

Harbor reached her hand toward Kelsey. Kelsey obliged. "Thank you for everything. I'm sorry I didn't get a chance to try on anything."

"Darlin', don't you worry about a thing," Kelsey said and winked. She walked over to a dress rack and pulled down a garment bag. She handed the bag to Ahmad. "I think the creations your mother and I picked out this morning will be perfect for your sister's big day."

Harbor stammered over her words, "I...I'm not sure. My mother and I aren't exactly on the same page about fashion." *Or anything at all,* Harbor wanted to add.

Kelsey hugged Harbor. "I think you'll be surprised," she said, then turned her attention to Ahmad. "Maud, I trust you will take good care of my new friend. If you don't," Kelsey said and did not have to finish her thought.

"Slow down with the threats, Cuz," Ahmad said as he opened the door to allow Harbor to walk out. "Harbor knows she's good with me."

Harbor smiled and offered a final wave to Kelsey. There was a list of things in her life she was not sure of, but Ahmad was right. She never doubted she was all good in his presence.

5

Ahmad was so sweet during and after Harbor's meltdown at Kelsey's that she wanted to do something special for him, like take him out for dinner or hit up some of their old hotspots, but her emotional account refused to cash another check. After leaving Kelsey's, Ahmad reluctantly dropped her off at the house. Harbor had to pinky promise to meet him for a secret assignment tomorrow.

Truth be told, strong-arming her with grade school tactics was unnecessary. Harbor had made up her mind she was going to spend every minute she could with Ahmad. The more time she spent with Ahmad, the less time she would have to make nice with her mother until they found themselves walking Patrice down the aisle.

Neither promise would be hard to keep, Harbor told herself as she sat in the parlor with her feet tucked beneath her on an early twentieth-century style loveseat. Ahmad seemed bound and determined for them to reconnect. Elizabeth, the two-time no-show, seemed just as determined to find herself in any space that did not include Harbor. The thought that her mother could not stand to be in the same space with her could drive Harbor to another fit of tears. She was not going out like that again...at least not twice in one day.

She needed an escape. An escape, for Harbor, always came between the pages of a good book. When she and Elizabeth were in the middle of one of their battles, Harbor would grab a book off the library shelf. Any book would do. She would lock herself in her room until her mind cleared and the protagonist completed a triumphant journey. Today was no different, except Harbor did not feel like being trapped in her room. And she doubted her mother would come home from whatever had stolen her attention anytime soon.

Harbor looked at the book jacket and smiled. She held one of her favorite books in her hands. The title gave a clue to what she needed in that moment...*Sense and Sensibility*. *This is exactly what I need*, Harbor told herself. She opened the book and began to read.

"Girl, get up!"

Harbor heard the shrill, demanding voice, but she did not know where the sound was coming from. Was somebody shaking her? Harbor felt her body rocking back and forth. She felt nauseous like she had on that stupid birthday cruise Patrice sent her on last year. She hated cruises. The rocking increased.

Oh, God, am I going overboard? I can't swim. Death by drowning is the worst.

The final shake was her undoing. Harbor jumped up from the loveseat, nearly falling off.

She felt herself being pushed back onto the safety of the boat...uh, loveseat. When she turned around, she saw Patrice's wide, corny grin, smiling back at her.

"What is wrong with you? "Harbor asked, shoving Patrice's "helping" hands away. "I was reading." She looked around for the book. She found it at her feet.

Patrice snatched the book before Harbor could reach for it. "Yeah, like four hours ago," she commented, tossing the book to Harbor. "Girl, you were knocked out. We ate dinner and everything."

Harbor sat up straight, seeming to get her bearings. She fingered through her twist out. "I missed dinner?" She asked in a voice that was a touch beyond groggy. "Why didn't you wake me?"

Patrice not so graciously removed Harbor's feet from the loveseat and plopped herself down. "Promise, I tried. But Ms. Amelia told me to 'leave that child be,' so that's what I did."

"Understood," was all Harbor could say. When Ms. Amelia gave clear instructions, not following her directive equated to mutiny. "Did y'all at least save me a plate?"

"In the fridge," Patrice stated matter-of-factly. "Ms. Amelia made your plate before anybody else could touch the food."

Harbor smiled. Ms. Amelia always had her back. She yawned and stretched like a newborn. "So, what else did I miss? Did Mom find her way home?"

"Safe and sound," Patrice responded. "Apparently, she was as tired as you because she went to her room right after dinner."

Harbor rolled her eyes. "So, I'm guessing her business must have been super taxing," she stated as fact, not even attempting to hide the sarcasm in her voice. She was so done being manipulated by her mother.

Patrice laid her hand on Harbor's knee. She gave her sister a look that resembled something between sympathy and truth. "Look, Sis, I'm going to tell you something I know you don't want to hear."

"Then don't tell me," Harbor said and stood. "I don't want to hear another list of excuses that gives Mom a pass for bad behavior."

Patrice stood as well. She took Harbor's hand. "Look, Girl, you need to give Mom a break. She's not perfect, but neither are you." Patrice placed her hand squarely on her hips. "Y'all need to figure this thing out. I'm not doing this on-again, off-again trip down drama lane. Especially not during my wedding week."

Harbor glared at her baby sister. Why couldn't Patrice see *she* was not the issue in this mother-daughter debacle? Harbor had spent a lifetime walking on eggshells because she knew how sensitive Patrice was about strife and tension. She would do anything to appease her baby sister.

Amendment...was doing anything for her, including putting up with this no-show foolishness.

"Did Mom tell you she stood me up?" Harbor blurted out in a voice that sounded more crushed than confident. She hated that her mother's shenanigans could affect her this much, but they did. "Twice she was a no-show."

Patrice laid a gentle hand on Harbor's shoulder. "I won't say another word. Except, I'm sorry, Sis."

Harbor shrugged. "It's not a big deal. Par for the course."

"Well, you mentioned it, so it must be a big deal," Patrice replied. "Okay, last thing. I promise."

Harbor snorted. Patrice's last thing was a long string of just one last thing. "I'm listening," she said.

"Good, because both of y'all are getting way too old to ignore all this emotional baggage," Patrice said like some kind of authority. "It's unhealthy."

Harbor almost choked. "'Emotional baggage.' I see someone has been watching daytime television again."

"Zero shame. It's very inspiring. And you know I'm right. It's time for y'all to fix your stuff."

Harbor waved dismissively, picked up her book, and left the parlor. Patrice followed. The click and clack of her five-inch stilettos, tapping their way across the marble floor, followed Harbor across the room.

Patrice ran the last few feet to catch up with Harbor. "Okay, enough mama talk. How was your day with Ahmad? Tell me everything."

Is she swooning? Harbor was almost sure she heard a distinct swoon in Patrice's voice. When she reached the kitchen, Harbor pulled a container from the fridge and tossed it in the microwave. She didn't bother taking off the lid. Harbor knew whatever Ms. Amelia cooked would be just what she needed to fill her empty tummy and soothe her weary soul.

When the microwave played its little "I'm ready" melody, Harbor took the container out and sat at the island. She blessed her food. Delight radiated through her core when she realized Ms. Amelia had prepared chicken and shrimp enchiladas. After her first bite, Harbor's eyes nearly rolled back in her head. *Too good.* Any issue with Ms. Amelia for trying to set her up with Ahmad this morning was forgiven. Harbor could not think of one thing she would hold against Ms. Amelia after a meal that made her belly do a happy dance.

Halfway through her last enchilada, she realized Patrice was still seated across from her, staring her down like some creepy stalker from a chick flick. "Okay, weirdo," Harbor began as she tossed the last bite of goodness into her mouth. "Can I eat in peace?"

Patrice slid a bottle of water across the island to Harbor. "I can't believe I just watched you inhale that. Take a breath, take a drink, then spill the tea. Add a dollop of sugar and a splash of cream. I want details, Honey."

Harbor took her sweet time taking a sip of her water. Telling Patrice about her day with Ahmad, which included an epic melt-down, did not rank high on her list of things to do. She made sure to screw the lid on the bottle of water good and tight before she said, "It was nice."

Patrice threw up her French-manicured fingernails in protest. "I can get nice from a cartoon. I need facts. Give me all the five-year sep-aration tension you got."

Harbor laughed and rolled her eyes. "All you need to know is that Ahmad is still a really good guy. I'm glad we had a chance to hang out today."

"A really good guy that you would be a fool to walk away from...again," Patrice said, giving Harbor an I-dare-you-to-challenge-me stare down.

Harbor stood and grabbed her water bottle. She walked toward the living room, yelling over her shoulder, "Good night, Sis."

"We could make this a double wedding," Patrice yelled when Harbor was halfway up the stairs. "Just say the word."

"Goodnight, Sis," Harbor responded, breaking into hysterical laughter as she closed her bedroom door.

***

Harbor wrongly assumed the extended nap she'd taken earlier that day would be a good sign she would get a decent night's rest. She was so wrong. Each time Harbor closed her eyes, she saw Elizabeth running away from her or Ahmad running to her. She'd nearly smothered Theodore Goodnight as she held the furry little guy in a death grip to give her something to hold onto through the night besides her racing thoughts.

When Harbor woke up a little after nine the next morning, she knew Patrice was right about one thing. She and Elizabeth needed to talk. *But not today*, Harbor decided when she checked the time on her phone. She had just enough time to pull herself together in her standard black tee, jeans rolled at the cuffs, and red sneakers before Ahmad showed up for this little surprise.

What tricks did Ahmad have up his sleeve today? Wedding business perhaps, or something personal he'd cooked up so they could spend another afternoon together. Hopefully, this little excursion would not end with Harbor crying because something else in her life went off the rails.

Harbor gave herself a once-over in her full-length mirror. "Good enough," she said, grabbing her backpack from the lavender settee beneath her window. On her way out the door, Harbor saluted Theodore. "See you later, fella."

When she reached the bottom of the staircase, Harbor slowed her pace. She heard voices coming from the parlor. Her mother and Ms. Amelia talked in hush tones about who knows what. Not her concern.

Standing still as a statue, Harbor waited on the bottom step. The one thing she knew how to do was sneak out of the house without her mother being the wiser. Elizabeth, perpetually caught up in her own thing, rarely used her mommy-radar to catch Harbor in the act of committing random foolishness back in the day.

Harbor needed a distraction. The head-to-head discussion, taking place feet away from her in the parlor, should have functioned as the perfect cover for Harbor's escape. But her stupid phone and the *When Can I See You* ringtone she'd set for Ahmad had other ideas. She needed to change that ringtone ASAP and put her phone back on Do Not Disturb, which was always standard operating procedure.

Harbor tried to stop the offending back-to-back text notifications, but the damage had been done. She heard Amelia's classic on-the-job loafers and her mother's sensible pumps walking out of the parlor and up to her in quick fashion.

She stole a glance at her phone while the women were en route.

Ahmad: *Morning, Tink. Be there in 5.*

Harbor: *Meet you outside.*

As the dynamic duo entered the foyer, Harbor tossed the phone in her pocket.

She looked up to see her mother, who was impeccably dressed for a day of leisure if Harbor guessed, giving her a quizzical look. *Not off-brand*, Harbor thought. Now, Ms. Amelia's usually jovial expression turned upside down into a frown, screamed something was off. Harbor decided to make her escape before she stumbled into this snare.

She hopped off the bottom step, walked the few steps over to the door, and pulled it open. A quick perusal of the driveway confirmed Ahmad was still a few minutes away. Harbor kept the door propped open with her foot and turned around to face her accusers.

"Good morning," Harbor said, looking from her mother to Ms. Amelia. "On my way out with Ahmad. Wedding stuff. See y'all later." She knew the pep in her voice sounded a little fake, but that was the best she could do, especially at no moment's notice.

Elizabeth offered Harbor her I-don't-want-to-make-a-scene smile. "I thought we could have breakfast this morning. Just the two of us." She walked toward Harbor tentatively, stopping just before reaching her daughter. "I asked Amelia to make all your favorite things."

Harbor turned to face Elizabeth and could do nothing but stare. The nerve of this woman to expect her to drop everything because *she* had finally decided Harbor was worth spending time with.

Wow. Was Elizabeth truly oblivious to her lifelong practice of neglect, Harbor wondered? Was her mother honestly unaware of the emotional angst she inflicted on Harbor every time she opened her mouth? Elizabeth Wilson was a smart and savvy woman. Could she be that dense?

Impossible. Every act of neglect, every slight, everything her mother did or said was done with intent.

For half a second, Harbor considered letting another round of thoughtless actions slide, but she couldn't. Not today.

She cleared her throat. "Ms. Amelia made breakfast for me yesterday, and it was delicious. *Ahmad* and I enjoyed all of my favorites. I don't think asking her for a do-over is fair because you...." Harbor let her final thoughts trail off when she caught the pleading look in Ms. Amelia's eyes.

Without saying a word, the older woman instructed Harbor to take one for the team. *What team?* #TeamWilson did not exist. Harbor wanted to scream at how ludicrous this entire scene was. Did her mother expect Ms. Amelia to recreate a playlist of her favorite breakfast items for a second day? *Not happening.*

Harbor stole another peek outside. *He's here.*

When Ahmad parked, Harbor waved and smiled with a grin she hoped didn't appear as desperate as she felt. She hoped her expression conveyed, "So glad to see you, friend," and not "Get me out of this, now!"

Harbor turned to face Elizabeth. "Ahmad is here. I have to go," she said, adding a flourish toward the door.

Harbor wished she hadn't turned back to look at her mother. Elizabeth's usually erect back, which was the definition of regal, seemed to slowly relax into a...slouch. Was her mother slouching? *That couldn't be right.* Elizabeth Wilson did not slouch.

When Harbor dared a glance toward Ms. Amelia, she got exactly what she had expected...a look of disappointment that could make a grown woman cry. Wait, she was a grown woman. But not grown enough to stand up to her granny of the heart, Ms. Amelia. Going down that path would not end well.

She needed to get out of this house. Harbor turned to leave but stopped just before crossing the threshold.

"Maybe we can do lunch or dinner tomorrow," Elizabeth suggested rather than demanded. "We should probably coordinate before the wedding."

Coordinate what? The only *thing* they needed to coordinate was to show up for Patrice on the day of to make sure baby girl arrived at the altar safe and sound. No, Harbor would not put herself out there again. Playing the back-and-forth game with Elizabeth had run its course.

Well, Mom, Harbor thought. *Callous actions have unintended consequences.* "I don't want to keep Ahmad waiting," she said as an afterthought on her way out the door.

As Harbor walked up to Ahmad's jeep, she prayed the sinking feeling in her stomach was a byproduct of missing her usual meet and greet with a bowl of honey nut oatmeal and not a nudge from the Holy Spirit to give into Elizabeth's request. If that was the case and God wanted her to extend another olive branch, she could not do that. Not yet, anyway.

Harbor's on-again-off-again relationship with God was her own doing, and she knew it. God would prompt her to do something she was not inclined to do, like offer her mother forgiveness, and she would present God, in return, a few counteroffers.

Harbor figured that hopping on a plane and returning to Norfolk to spend a week in her childhood home after five years was enough. *It had to be enough.* Even as the thought formed in Harbor's heart, she had been in a relationship with God long enough to know His will would be done. How long, winding, and thorny the journey ended up being was Harbor's choice.

Ms. Amelia, in her no-nonsense way, told Harbor once she was "the most hard-headed child God ever did fashion," after she'd gotten caught sneaking out of her room to go to a senior party. Actually, Ms. Amelia had given Harbor the hard-headed child speech more times than she cared to remember. She could have disagreed with the assessment, but her words were spot on, like nearly every piece of commentary Ms. Amelia freely provided.

Harbor had never learned the art of getting it right the first time. If she had, she would already be Mrs. Ahmad Ferebee instead of his long-lost fiancé that had been MIA for the last five years.

Harbor looked toward the house. She was probably trippin' but thought she saw one of the lacy living room sheers shift from side to side like someone had released it after peeking outside. Harbor buckled her seat belt and turned to Ahmad.

"So, where's this surprise, Mr. Ferebee?" She asked. "Is this a Patrice and Colin thing for the wedding?" She added slowly. "If it is, I'm cool with that. Just need to get my mind prepared for business instead of pleasure."

Did I just say that? I just said that.

Ahmad rubbed his goatee, seeming to consider something. He double-tapped the steering wheel, nodded, then started the car. "So, if this is strictly personal, you'd be down?" He asked with more than a bit of doubt, weaving its way through his smooth baritone.

"Maybe," Harbor responded. She hunched her shoulders nonchalantly. She wanted to throw her hands up in delight but dialed it back. Ahmad's surprises were always epic. The last surprise he'd thrown Harbor's way brought back bittersweet memories.

Ahmad had taken Harbor to two of her favorite spots. First, they went on an early morning stroll at the Virginia Beach Oceanfront, just as the sun was rising. They'd walked hand in hand along the shore, enjoying being in each other's presence. Then, she and Ahmad enjoyed a divine crab cake lunch at a local diner with a 1970's vibe. He wasn't a seafood fanatic like Harbor, but he'd said he wanted to do something special for her. And Harbor *had* felt special. Ahmad was good at doing that, she reminisced.

To Harbor's surprise and dismay, Ahmad had also booked them for a night cruise. Harbor was not about the cruise lifestyle, but being with Ahmad anytime, anywhere was worth the wobbly legs and queasy tummy.

At some point, after they'd enjoyed a romantic meal and snuggled on the deck as the ship made its way around the Elizabeth River, Ahmad shocked Harbor when he proposed, with a hundred or so onlookers oohing and aahing over their young love.

Harbor regretted the beautiful memory was just that...a memory. Several weeks ago, Patrice had sent her a link to a news story about the ship. The regal vessel had been decommissioned after thirty years of service. It was essentially put out to pasture and deemed useless like so many other things in her previous life.

There were no do-overs in life, Harbor recognized as fact. The best she could hope for at this point was that she and Ahmad remained a part of each other's lives forever and ever, even as friends. The thought of relegating her relationship with Ahmad to the friend zone left Harbor with an empty feeling in the pit of her soul.

Friends...boo!

"Where to, Sir?" Harbor asked, tossing her feet on the dash. Regardless of the chaos battling in her mind and heart, she would put every ounce of herself into enjoying this day.

Ahmad pulled out of the driveway. "You trust me?" He asked with a smile that hinted at something neither of them would ever forget.

Harbor smiled and closed her eyes. "I do," she responded with a lightness in her voice she had forgotten even existed.

***

Ahmad knew at some point he would have to wake Harbor. She had fallen into a deep sleep almost as soon as he'd pulled out of her Burch Creek neighborhood. Ahmad hoped this impromptu excursion would give Harbor the rest she desperately needed. When she came rushing out of the house that morning, Ahmad could almost feel the stress she wore like a tattered robe that had seen better days, but getting rid of it was hard, if not impossible, to do.

Ahmad checked his watch. It was a little after 1. Since it was a clear summer day, they still had plenty of time to do what he had dubbed "The Harbor Tour." Each place he'd chosen to take her was on her list of want-tos and some days. Ahmad doubted Harbor had taken the time to do anything she truly wanted to do for a long time. Maybe he couldn't give her the world just yet. He could give Harbor a chance just to breathe.

Ahmad found an R&B station and turned the volume down to almost a whisper. He closed his eyes briefly, about to take a few winks when Harbor began to stir. She rolled her shoulders, worked out the kinks, then smiled and opened her eyes. This was a sight he could get used to.

"Hey," Harbor said groggily. She stretched and yawned, then gave her twist out a bit of a shake.

"Hey, to you too," Ahmad said, playfully nudging her shoulder. "How did you rest?"

Harbor peered out of her window at the groups of people walking down the sidewalk. Some wore business attire. Others looked like they were taking a day trip, just enjoying the sights. The building they were parked across the street from looked familiar with its stately form and several sets of stairs, but she couldn't place it.

"Where are we?" Harbor asked as she searched for the hard mint candy she always kept in her bag. If her stale breath was any indication, she had slept for longer than a minute. She popped the mint in her mouth and savored the refreshing taste, peering at the building with narrowed eyes. At that moment, something beautiful clicked in Harbor's heart.

She turned to Ahmad, who had the biggest and cheesiest grin on his face. "Sir, please confirm we are at the Library of Congress." Harbor squealed. This time, she could not contain her happy dance. She unbuckled her seat belt and twisted back and forth to a nineties R&B tune like the catchy song was written just for this moment. And maybe it was because Harbor could not stop this groove if she wanted to. So, she didn't.

When the song ended, Harbor faced Ahmad. "This is at least a four-hour drive from Norfolk to D.C. Please tell me I was not asleep that long."

"I'd be lying if I said otherwise." Ahmad laughed, cutting off the radio. "I stopped for gas and snacks in Richmond. Then, I had kind of an abnormally long conversation with the old guy parked beside us who invited us to his niece's wedding at the end of August in Chesapeake. And I laid on my horn several times fighting D.C. traffic, all without you waking up."

"No!" Harbor groaned. "I should say I'm sorry, but I am so not." She placed her hand over Ahmad's hand and gave it a little squeeze. The shiver that raced through Harbor's body at his touch was real and scary, and everything she'd missed about Ahmad's nearness over the last five years.

She slid her hand back to the safety of her lap and gave herself a half second to wonder if Ahmad felt even a tenth of what she was feeling. If he did and allowed himself to feel all his feelings, the rest of this week would be more of the unexpected for them both.

Ahmad turned off the engine. "You ready?" He asked. "Days a wasting."

Harbor shook her head. "You are so country. And yes, I am ready."

She could take or leave having her door opened by *a* man but not *this* man. If Ahmad didn't make his way to her side of the car to open her door, something was either off with him, the situation, or the world. Harbor laughed to herself as Ahmad opened her door and offered her his hand.

"My lady, your tour of all things Dewey Decimal awaits."

Harbor grinned and stepped out of the jeep. Only a man who truly got who she was and appreciated all things Harbor Wilson would drive more than two-hundred miles out of his way to take her to a place she had wanted to visit for several years but never made the time to do so.

Ahmad Ferebee, Harbor thought as they walked hand in hand across Independence Avenue. *Why did I ever let you go?*

6

Harbor would have been more than satisfied if their D.C. visit had begun and ended at the Library of Congress. Because Ahmad was Ahmad, there was so much more in store. After they'd scoured the Library of Congress up and down, inside and out, and absorbed all the historical jewels waiting to be discovered, Harbor and Ahmad took the nearly hours-long walk to the Martin Luther King, Jr. Memorial. Although Harbor had wanted to visit the site in 2011, she relished having time to take a slow walk around the serene space with Ahmad.

Whenever the familiar feeling of guilt tried to overtake her about neglecting wedding business or leaving Elizabeth standing in the foyer looking like a lost child, Harbor stomped the all too familiar feeling back into its place. She was certain when her head hit the pillow that night, she would have plenty of time to mull over everything she could have and should have done.

When they reached the Martin Luther King, Jr. Memorial, dozens of other tourists were visiting the site. But even as tourists came and went during the hour she and Ahmad walked and quietly contemplated, Harbor noticed how calm and peaceful the environment felt. Among the group of strangers, there was a reverence for the man who used his words and actions to make changes that continued to reverberate around the world.

Harbor hoped her life's legacy would positively impact the world. Heck, a minor impact on her inner circle would suffice. She had no idea how that would happen when most of her relationships were on the outs.

When Ahmad said he wanted to take her to another place before leaving D.C., Harbor *almost* told him she would rather stay at the Memorial until it was time to head home. She did not want to relinquish the peace she felt in this place that embraced her like an auntie she hadn't seen in a long, long while.

After Harbor had given herself a mini pep talk about coming back to visit the Memorial soon, she'd placed her hand in Ahmad's. She allowed him to escort her to their next destination. As they strolled around the city, encountering both beauty and want, her eyes feasted on one mural after another. *What a sight.* Each mural was unique and each inspiring, making Harbor believe for just a moment these masterpieces were created solely for her enjoyment. *Who knows, maybe they were*, Harbor thought when they walked back to Ahmad's jeep.

She didn't want this day to end. She didn't want to return home to the mess she all but ran away from this morning. Every moment of her time with Ahmad had been so easy, so peaceful. *Amendment...*it was easy, peaceful, and one hundred percent no drama until they'd gotten on the road after rolling through a drive-through for chicken strips and fries.

After they'd dipped their way through every sauce combination imaginable, loaded up on too much sweet tea, and played the license plate game from D.C. to Fredericksburg, Ahmad got the brilliant idea that it was the perfect time for them to talk. *Talk about what?*

They had been in each other's company for most of the day. Granted, Harbor was knocked out when they started this little field trip, but she was fully engaged once they had gotten to D.C. and started their city tour. *What else did this man want to talk about?*

And then it happened. Ahmad morphed into Mr. Let's Get Down to Business in a snap. Sadly, Mr. Good Times Tour Guide had said his goodbyes at the drive-through. Harbor was not impressed if this was God's way of getting her to take an overdue trip down memory lane with her former fiancé.

Lord, I just need more time, Harbor almost begged. After the wedding and finding her way back to Atlanta and to the solitude of her one-bedroom condo, Harbor would embark on the emotional deep dive everyone wanted her to take. She just wasn't ready to do it now. Maybe she never would be.

Ahmad turned down the radio and turned on the windshield wipers when it began to rain. His grip on the steering wheel was intense. Ahmad was not an intense man, but something in him had changed after spending the day with Harbor. He knew she was not ready to discuss their break-up five years ago if that's what it was.

After her father's funeral, Harbor had taken off for parts unknown. All his calls went straight to voicemail. The hundreds of texts Ahmad had sent apparently did not warrant a reply because the woman he thought he would spend the rest of his life with completely ghosted him.

Ahmad willed himself to loosen his grip on the steering wheel when he checked his side mirror and moved back into the right lane. He was in no rush to take Harbor home, giving her another opportunity to avoid talking to him.

Ahmad glanced at Harbor, who looked like she was about to jump out of the car at the next opportunity. Ahmad would have respected Harbor's wishes and backed off at any other point in their on-again, off-again relationship that took flight during their junior year in high school. He would have given in to her I-don't-want-to-talk-about-this hard line in the sand. Not today. Today, Ahmad needed answers that were long overdue.

"Tink," he began, hoping the nickname only shared between the two of them would open her heart to his request. "Please, can we talk?"

Harbor continued to stare out of the window. Looking at the dancing rain slide down the window was a welcomed albeit slight reprieve from this come to Jesus with Ahmad. It took every ounce of Harbor's always-at-the-ready self-will not to word vomit every thought she'd had about their failed relationship over the last five years.

She had blamed herself. She'd blamed Ahmad. In her less-than-stellar moments, Harbor even blamed global warming, inflation, and the price of oil for their demise. Did any of that make sense? Absolutely not. Did her off-the-rail thoughts give her an excuse not to take a deep dive into why she walked away from Ahmad without an explanation? Absolutely.

Harbor noticed the rain was picking up as traffic was slowing down to something close to a crawl. If she didn't have some good sense, she would have believed that Ahmad orchestrated the wacky weather and untimely traffic jam to force her hand on this thing. Harbor hated being forced to do anything she did not want to do.

Like mother, like daughter, Harbor thought.

She shifted her body to face Ahmad. Harbor tried to decipher what this look was on that beautiful face. Tightly clenched jaw muscles would not do.

Before Harbor could talk herself out of stroking his barely stubbled jawline, she reached over and did just that. She felt his muscles relax beneath her touch.

Harbor smiled to herself, triumphant. She was crossing some invisible line, and she knew it. Harbor began slowly withdrawing her hand when Ahmad captured her hand in his. His eyes never left the road and the traffic that barely moved.

Harbor looked at their intertwined hands and sighed. She loved this man. What was her problem?

"What do you want to know?"

"Everything," Ahmad said.

Everything. That was off the table. Ahmad, ever the optimist, had no idea what type of minefield he was walking into by asking Harbor to bare her soul on this slow drive back to Norfolk. She knew taking a trip down "Everything Lane" would send Ahmad running fast and far. *Poor sap has no idea what he's getting into with this little intervention*, Harbor thought.

"Look, I don't think I can. I just," Harbor began, hearing her words fall out of her mouth in a jumbled mess. Having this man hold her hand in such a gentle and loving grip while trying to explain the unexplainable would not work. So, Harbor kindly removed her hand and the rest of herself back to the safety of her side of the car. She folded her arms across her chest before she said, "I can't give you what you want, Ahmad."

Ahmad placed his other hand back on the steering wheel just as traffic began to pick up and the quick-moving storm began to cease. The storm brewing inside of him was just beginning to rev up.

"Tink, are you serious? You haven't given me anything," Ahmad began in a voice that spoke of his pent-up frustrations. "You know you are really good at telling me what you don't have and what you can't give me. But don't you think five years is enough time for you to have figured out what went wrong? We were good, Tink, and then we weren't. You walked away from me...from us." He ran a hand through his locs. "You owe me an explanation."

"I'm not doing this with you right now, Ahmad." Harbor adjusted her seat. She let it recline as far back as it would go. "We had a good day. Let's leave it at that." Harbor closed her eyes and released a long sigh. "Goodnight, Mr. Ferebee."

Ahmad let out a long, slow sigh of his own. Now that traffic was beginning to move, he hopped into the left lane and increased his speed. Gone were any hopes of turning this trip into a confession session. He glanced quickly at his "sleeping" ex-fiancé/friend/first love. What was Harbor to him?

"Woman, you are incredibly infuriating," Ahmad said under his breath. "Why do I torture myself?" He knew the answer. He'd always known the answer.

Because I love you. Ahmad accepted the admission as a fact. *But you have got to let me love you. Lord, please help me.*

***

Ahmad and Harbor arrived at the house in record time. The four-hour journey from D.C. to Norfolk was shaved down by at least thirty minutes if Harbor had to guess. Unlike the unexpected trip to D.C., Harbor did not enjoy even a moment's rest on the trip home. Although her eyes were clamped shut, Harbor's thoughts were spinning out of control like a compact car on an icy mountain road.

She'd probably damaged her relationship with Ahmad more in the last few hours than she had in the past five years. At least when she was in Atlanta doing her thing outside of the presence of her friends or family, the status of each of her relationships remained firmly grounded in the status quo. Nothing was fixed, but nothing was irrevocably broken either.

Harbor was confident she would never win a prize for making proactive relationship decisions, which was a completely acceptable way to exist as far as she was concerned. And that is precisely what she was doing...existing. Ahmad was challenging her to live again without being saddled by her pains from the past. And he seemed ready, willing, and able to come along for the ride no matter how bumpy the journey might become.

When Ahmad pulled into the driveway, Harbor expected them to sit in awkward silence for several long moments before one cried "Auntie." But that's not how it went down. As soon as Ahmad put the jeep in park, he hopped out of the car and walked swiftly to Harbor's door. He opened her door and then took two large steps backward.

Harbor groaned when she witnessed Ahmad's over-the-top effort to create space between them. She couldn't prolong what was beginning to feel like agony any longer. Harbor put her arms through her backpack and stepped from the car.

She rocked back and forth on her sneakers before she said, "Thanks for...everything."

Ahmad moved to take a step toward her, then stepped back into his place. He shoved his hands in his back pockets. "Of course," he said. "I'll probably swing by tomorrow. I think Colin and Patrice have some things they want us to do for the wedding. Maybe I'll see you then."

Maybe? "Sure," Harbor said quickly, moving swiftly toward the front door. For some strange and stupid reason, she expected Ahmad to follow her. He always followed her. Not today. When Harbor turned around to wave, he was already standing at his car door, about to slide his six-foot frame behind the wheel.

"Night," she whispered.

She thought he responded, but maybe that was wishful thinking on her part.

When Harbor walked into the house, everyone seemed to be snuggly tucked away in their beds for the night. The last thing she needed was to jump into another conversation doomed to fail. She needed a long, hot shower and a little talk with Jesus. If He did not have the answers she desperately needed, no one would, especially at this hour.

She checked her watch. It was just after midnight. She could knock on Patrice's door for a bit of girl chat and hope her baby sister would not pop off on her for disturbing her beauty rest. *Not worth it.* That girl needed at least ten hours every night, Harbor thought and laughed. No, she would not incur Patrice's wrath tonight.

Harbor headed upstairs to her room. When she opened the door and turned on the light, she tossed her backpack down and kicked off her shoes. Harbor headed toward the bathroom to let a lilac and lavender lather party wash all her troubles away. A movement on the settee caught her attention.

"Mom?"

"Can we talk?" Elizabeth asked in something close to a whisper. *Okay, God. I hear you.*

***

As hard as Harbor's head was at times, even she could clearly see her long-standing policy of avoiding unpacking her emotional baggage was coming to a quick and decisive close. Elizabeth rarely stepped over the threshold into Harbor's room without an explicit invitation. So, whatever they were about to get into was going down tonight or this morning if Harbor's watch was correct.

This was unprecedented territory for them both. Harbor walked to her bed and grabbed Theodore Goodnight from his comfy spot on her mound of pillows. She didn't know how much support the little guy could give her for this mother-daughter meet and greet, but she would take whatever she could get.

Knees drawn up to her chin with Theodore in a death grip between her knees, Harbor said, "I'm listening."

"Then I guess I'm talking," Elizabeth responded and stood. She walked over to sit on the edge of the queen size bed.

Harbor's eyes widened at the sight of *her* mother on *her* bed. When she was a child, she'd spent countless hours talking to Ms. Amelia on this very bed about a myriad of things, and it always felt natural. Their conversations were sometimes easy, always challenging, and sandwiched in love. But being in her room with this pale pink robe, fuzzy slippers version of her mother unnerved her.

Lord, what is this? She stilled herself from moving further away from her mother.

Elizabeth fiddled with the belt on her robe, tying and untying the smooth fabric repeatedly before saying, "I hope one of the outfits Kelsey and I picked out for you will work for the wedding." She looked at the unopened garment bag hanging on the door.

Harbor's eyes followed Elizabeth's gaze to the door. "I guess we will see." Her response was flat, without a hint of enthusiasm. Harbor did not want to be that person, but Elizabeth "Lizzie" Wilson would have to work for this impromptu heart-to-heart.

"Did I ever tell you where your father and I met?"

Okay, abrupt subject change. Harbor shook her head. "Not that I recall."

A slow, deliberate smile worked its way to Elizabeth's perfectly-pink, glossed lips. "If you can believe it, your father and I met at a baseball game."

Harbor coughed. This was not one of those dainty, clear-your-throat-of-a-little-tickle coughs. No, this was a full-on coughing fit Harbor had to rein in before Elizabeth patted her on her back like she was a newborn. When Elizabeth stood to offer assistance, Harbor waved a hand to signal all was well.

She tried clearing her throat again with a little more success. "I'm good. I'm just surprised to hear you went to a baseball game," Harbor finally said, scooting back into the plush, stacked pillows behind her back. "Was this a blind date or some kind of bet?"

Elizabeth laughed. "No, and no," she responded with a lightness in her voice that rarely made an appearance, at least not around Harbor. "My roommate, Tonya, and I were about to lose our minds preparing for final exams a few weeks before graduation."

"You graduated from Bragston University, right?" Harbor asked, knowing the answer but wanting to add something to her longest conversation with her mother in years.

"I did," Elizabeth said and nodded with pride. "I loved being at Bragston, but we were tired after four years of keeping our heads in the books. So, Tonya suggested we go to a baseball game."

"And you agreed? Just like that." Harbor found that hard to believe.

Elizabeth's eyes took on a faraway look as memories of her past took center stage in her mind. "Actually, I did. I am not a baseball fan, but I wanted to try something new. So, Tonya and I showed up for the first game played at Harbor Love Stadium on opening day. Truth be told, we had so much fun that day."

Harbor smiled. She couldn't remember hearing her mother say she'd had fun doing anything. And at a baseball game, for goodness' sake. "So, how did you meet Daddy?"

"Your father was attending Tanson College and about to graduate with a business degree. He was also working at the concession stand at Harbor Love Stadium to make some extra money while he completed his studies. When I first saw him, I don't know. Something just clicked for me. I guess with him too. He asked for my phone number, and after that, we were inseparable."

Harbor did a bit of quick math in her head. "So, you guys were both seniors about to graduate in 1993 when you started dating?

Starting a new relationship when you are about to start your life seems like a lot. Why would you do that?"

Elizabeth did not miss a beat. "Because we were in love and wanted to start our lives together."

Harbor could not help but compare her mother and father's relationship and her failed attempt at a life with Ahmad.

If she had stayed in the area after her father's funeral, she would have graduated from Tanson like her father and married Ahmad not long after. They would have set up a life in Norfolk or Virginia Beach, had a couple of kids, and more than likely fallen into disrepair like her parents. And she would have eventually become the younger, disengaged version of her mother she never wanted to become.

Leaving was the right thing to do.

"Mom, why are you telling me this?"

Elizabeth pushed her slight frame onto the bed a little more. She turned to face Harbor, looking at her oldest daughter for a long moment before she said, "You may not believe this, but I know what kind of mother I have been to you. I never gave you what you needed from me." Elizabeth reached her hand across the bed toward Harbor, then slowly withdrew it.

"When your father and I married, we had such hopes for the kind of life we would live and the kind of parents we would be. We were going to kiss all the boo-boos together, show up for every parent-teacher meeting together, and be the best basketball parents that ever showed up to a game on a Sunday afternoon together." Elizabeth wiped at a stray tear. Then another.

"But after you were born and your father's real estate business started to take off, something got lost in translation between us." Elizabeth shook her head, seemingly trying to make sense of days long since passed. "No, it wasn't something. It was me. *I* got lost in translation. And then I got mad at your father. No, I was furious. We were supposed to be in this thing...this life together. And then suddenly, we weren't."

The last thing Harbor wanted to do at that moment was to feel compassion for the mother who never cared for her with the intense joy that a mother should...but she did. She had loved her father more than anything. Bradford Wilson was a good man, and Harbor would not trade her relationship with him for anything in the world. But if she allowed herself to take an honest, big-girl assessment of her childhood, Harbor would admit that her father spent maybe twenty percent of his time genuinely connecting with their family.

He was home long enough to make certain Elizabeth looked the part and that the house looked just so to impress the next potential client. Bradford Wilson spent every ounce of his time building a mini real estate empire that ultimately sent him to an early grave. *Crazy.* But none of that explained why her mother was the way she was.

"Why didn't you meet me for breakfast on Tuesday or at Kelsey's?" Harbor asked before she could force her mouth into silent submission. She wanted to make herself believe the slight was no big deal, but it was. "I waited for you."

Elizabeth stood. She walked around to Harbor's side of the bed. She sat only inches from her daughter. "You needed time."

Harbor looked at her mother, confused. "I don't understand. Time for what?"

Elizabeth took hold of Harbor's hand. Harbor let her. "You needed time to be with Ahmad. You needed time to talk to him again. To be with your best friend. To be with the man you love."

The iceberg encasing Harbor's heart and emotions began to thaw at a rapid pace. Her eyes filled with tears. She knew she loved Ahmad.

Always had. Always would. But Harbor had never heard her mother acknowledge that truth...at least not to her.

Elizabeth squeezed Harbor's hand. "You were all set to marry Ahmad when your father died. And I became impossible to live with." She knew Bradford's unexpected death was just another excuse to solidify her aloof behavior toward her child. "I am so, so sorry for all my missteps. Every single one of them. I was angry at your father for forgetting about me, and I took it out on you. That was never my intention."

Elizabeth raised Harbor's chin with her finger so that their eyes met. "When I found out I was pregnant with you, I...we were over the moon. You were our beautiful baby girl who reminded me of the love your father and I shared for one another."

"So, what changed?" Harbor asked, feeling a mingled sense of both sadness and relief.

Elizabeth withdrew her hands to her lap. "I changed," she said after a long, introspective moment. "I let bitterness about your father and what I wasn't getting from him consume me. I craved Bradford's attention. What I did not recognize was that you needed my attention. You needed me, Harbor. I wasn't there. For that, I am so, so sorry, my love."

My love.

Harbor's mind raced. All this time, she thought *she* was the issue. She believed if she could master how to sit like a lady, eat with the correct fork, or say just the right thing at a gathering of Elizabeth's socialite friends, her mother would find a way to love her.

Harbor never believed that being Harbor Monae Wilson, with all her quirks and flaws, would be enough. God, ever the patient Father, was showing her His truth in her childhood home, sitting next to a woman who was feeling less and less like a stranger. She was masterfully and uniquely made in His image regardless of what any other person believed...even her mother. But to know her mother actually loved her mattered. Something told Harbor it mattered more than she may ever understand.

Elizabeth swiped at another stream of tears and then looked at Harbor. "After your father died and you left, I was a mess. I cut off all social engagements for nearly a year, if you can believe it."

That was breaking news. Her mother must have been completely broken to cut off all her fancy friends and their grand adventures. Anytime Ms. Amelia or Patrice tried to update Harbor about how Elizabeth was faring, she "politely" declined a play-by-play of her mother's woes. At that point, she was trying and spectacularly failing to juggle her own angst. She had no interest in wading through Elizabeth's emotional minefield.

Harbor stifled a yawn. The long day and too many long-overdue revelations were getting to her. She had never been able to hang up until the wee hours, and it was showing.

Elizabeth stood. "You need your rest. It's been a long couple of days."

Harbor nodded. Still holding Theodore, she stood and walked with Elizabeth to her door. "Thanks."

Elizabeth touched Harbor's cheek. "You are so welcome," she said, opening the door. "Do you think we can try breakfast tomorrow? Well, this morning."

Because all of this get-to-know-you stuff was new and completely out of the blue, Harbor had to sit on the, "Absolutely not," response she would have given her mother before their breakthrough.

Did they have a breakthrough? Harbor marveled at God. *Look at You!*

"Sure. But let's not bother Ms. Amelia. We can go to Waffle Central or Baker's Best if that will work."

Elizabeth stepped into the hall. "I would love that," she said, turning to leave. Before she walked down the hall, Elizabeth turned back to Harbor and said, "When you were born, I told your father in no uncertain terms that we *were* naming you Harbor."

Harbor cocked her head. "Why? Harbor isn't exactly on the top ten list of girl names. Is it even a name?" Harbor looked sheepish. "No offense."

Elizabeth laughed. "None taken. I named you Harbor because I always wanted to remember how my story with your father began and where it began."

Harbor sighed. "Harbor Love Stadium," she whispered.

Elizabeth smiled. "See you in the morning."

For the first time in a lifetime, Harbor looked forward to seeing her mother in the morning.

7

The days leading up to the wedding resembled a tornado, barreling through a small Kansas town. Patrice and Colin's emotional highs and lows were on full display. They engaged in one too many drawn-out conversations about having a sit-down dinner or a buffet reception. And their "disagreements" about who loved whom more caused Harbor to pop anti-nausea meds way too often.

Patrice and Colin's pre-wedding drama smacked of one of those feel-good rom-coms Harbor rarely watched anymore since calling it quits with Ahmad. That was precisely why she had given the lovebirds a hard, not-gonna-happen pass when they'd suggested she and Ahmad join them for a movie date.

The last thing Harbor wanted was to watch made-for-tv couples fall in and out of love. Harbor had a sneaking suspicion Ahmad would not have the stomach for all that lovey-dovey nonsense either, which she could not confirm because she had not heard a peep out of that man.

At least she was making progress on the mommy front. Harbor willed herself to be fully present as she worked with her mother to plan an upscale event that lived up to the grandeur of a Wilson family gathering, even if they only had a couple of days to pull it off. For the life of her, Harbor could not understand how she had gone from not having a relationship with her mother or any form of communication to them helping Patrice pick out wedding dresses two days before the big event.

The bridge Harbor lovingly constructed to reach out to her mother apparently did not include an extension to reach Ahmad. It had been two days since their failed trip to the District of Columbia. Ahmad was playing the avoidance game like he was the original inventor and expected to receive lifetime royalties.

Harbor could not get that man to be in the same space with her for longer than it took her to say, "Hey, how are you doing?" Ahmad made a point of allowing himself to be whisked away by Colin for best man duties or to run some solo errand that kept him away from the house and away from Harbor.

Shopping for wedding dresses with her mother and Patrice had come as a welcomed reprieve for Harbor. Since Elizabeth had arranged with Kelsey to have a show of dresses at the house so they could take care of other wedding business, helping Patrice choose the perfect dress was as drama free as it could be with their tight deadline.

To see how effortlessly her mother kept calm while offering Patrice advice about a flattering neckline for the dress, texting the caterers about the precise moment to reveal the bounty of food to their guests, and battling Ms. Amelia over which China setting reflected the gold in Patrice's eyes, left Harbor speechless. The woman was an organizing beast, Harbor thought when she looked up to see Patrice walk into the parlor, wearing a fitted, princess wedding dress that hugged all her baby sister's numerous curves.

She's not my baby anymore, Harbor realized as she watched Patrice twirl back and forth in the full-length mirror.

"You look beautiful, Sis."

Patrice jumped up and down. "This is the one," she squealed in the highest pitch known to man. "This...is...the...one."

Harbor moved from the loveseat to stand behind Patrice. She put her arms around her baby sister, enveloping her in a hug. "It's the one. You look amazing. Colin is not going to know what to do with you, Girl."

"Oh, I'm sure that boy will figure it out," Amelia chimed in from her seat on the sofa beside Elizabeth. "I wouldn't worry none about that."

Harbor and Patrice broke out in schoolgirl laughter. Their giggles must have been infectious because even Elizabeth, who rarely acknowledged an off-color comment, let a small, dignified giggle escape. Elizabeth immediately covered her mouth with her hand. The gesture made Harbor smile.

Back in the day, her mother would have admonished Ms. Amelia or thrown a disapproving glare her way. Harbor began to understand how much of a genuine transition her mother had experienced since her father's death. She knew it would take time, effort, and much prayer to build a genuine mother-daughter relationship with Elizabeth, but this was a beautiful start.

"Ms. Amelia, you are too much." Harbor winked at the older woman. "I agree, Colin will know exactly what to do with his beautiful new bride."

"Indeed, I will," Colin's deep baritone sailed in through the foyer.

"Don't you dare come in here," Harbor demanded. She ran out of the parlor to run interference before the eager groom got a peek at his bride. When Harbor entered the foyer, she spotted Colin and Ahmad standing by the front door, holding garment bags. Harbor stole a quick glance at Ahmad. Of course, he looked as gorgeous as ever, but his standard jovial expression decided not to make an appearance.

We need to talk.

Harbor turned her attention to Colin, who wore the cheesy grin of a man in love. "What are y'all doing here? You told me you would text me before you came," she admonished with as much attitude in her voice as she could muster. But there was no point. How could she stay mad with a man that loved her sister without limits?

"Okay, listen up, brother-in-law-to-be." Harbor pointed to the garment bags. "Put those tuxedos or suits or whatever y'all have in those bags in the living room and skedaddle. Hit the bricks. Keep it moving."

Patrice yelled from the parlor, "I love you, baby!"

"I love you too, Boo!" Colin yelled back.

"Oh, please," Harbor and Ahmad objected in unison. They gave each other a quick side glance then both focused their attention on Colin.

Harbor took Colin's garment bag. "I'll take care of this. You need to go somewhere and do something. You will not see my sister in that stunning dress before Saturday."

Colin narrowed his eyes and grinned. "Yes, ma'am." He turned to Ahmad. "I guess we are getting kicked out, Bro."

"Pause," Harbor interrupted. "*You* are getting kicked out." She pointed to Ahmad. "He is coming with me." Harbor turned to walk into the living room without another word.

Colin hunched his shoulders before reaching for the door handle. "Good luck, man. You're going to need it."

Ahmad sighed, watching Harbor make her exit. He could not believe she just expected him to follow her. This woman always got her way. He should just leave and make her wait on him like he'd waited for her every day since she'd taken off. Ahmad felt Colin's hands on his shoulders, turning him toward the living room.

"Just go," Colin advised. "Do whatever you need to do to fix whatever this is before my wedding. Patrice and I do not do drama."

"That's right, Baby, tell him," Patrice yelled. "Not even low drama."

"Because we don't do drama at all," Patrice and Colin sang in unison.

Ahmad was done with this love fest. He could not do the math on how two people chose to plan a wedding in seven days equaled a low drama existence.

Impossible.

He waved a quick "goodbye" to Colin and headed toward the living room. His steps were purposeful but a little slower than his normal walking speed. Ahmad needed time to think about what he wanted to say to Harbor. What he *needed* to say to Harbor. As much as he wanted her to be forthcoming about her feelings, he also needed to lay all his cards on the table.

Harbor was placing Colin's suit in the closet when he arrived. Ahmad made his way over to the closet. "Thank you for keeping these here," he said, handing her the garment bag. His hand brushed her hand with the exchange. No matter how much time or space wedged its way between them because of misunderstandings or fear, Harbor's touch always felt like home. With Harbor, Ahmad *was* home.

Remembering his promise to keep as much space between them as possible, Ahmad walked toward a window on the other side of the living room that overlooked the lake. Sunlight danced playfully across the water, which helped to rein in his racing thoughts. Ahmad prayed a silent prayer that God would still his anxious heart and help both he and Harbor to hear one another.

Harbor walked over to the other side of the window. She took a cue from Ahmad and let the peace of the lake surround her before she spoke. "Ahmad, I don't have all the answers you need," Harbor began in a low voice. "But I will try."

"That's all I want."

Good, because that's all I've got.

Harbor knew trying to speak her piece was the best she could do, even for Ahmad. "I was scared."

The moment Ahmad's face registered a level of hurt she had never seen before, Harbor rushed to explain, "I wasn't scared of you, Ahmad," she said, noticing his jaw muscles relax. "When Daddy died, I saw my mom go all in with being bitter about her life and everything in her world."

Ahmad nodded. "Okay." He didn't understand where Harbor was going with this, but after five years of waiting, he would willingly take a slow walk with her on their journey.

Harbor shifted from one foot then to the other. "I didn't want to become like my mom. Well, like she was. Anyway, that's another story." Harbor's ability to form a cohesive thought was rapidly diminishing. She needed to get this out before she totally confused herself and Ahmad.

"When you asked me to marry you, I saw our life together, and it was beautiful. I envisioned all the good and all the blessings God had in store for our future. But after Daddy died, I freaked out because I knew I was letting bitterness take hold of me like it had with my mom. I was not the person I wanted to be. And I just...I couldn't do that to you. I couldn't do that to us." Tears welled up in Harbor's eyes. "So, I left."

Ahmad took a step toward Harbor, closing the space between them. He took her hand and wiped away a stray tear that finally found its way down her cheek. "Tink, when you left, you took a part of me with you. You were here, and then you were gone. I had no idea where you were or how to find you. That crushed me."

"I'm so sorry," Harbor responded in a low voice. She placed her hand on his heart. "I'm so, so sorry."

Ahmad nodded. He drew her hand to his lips and kissed her inner wrist. He grinned. "You know, I don't even know what you do for a living. And I couldn't get anything out of Patrice."

My girl.

"I'm a ghostwriter."

Ahmad's eyes widened. "Okay," he drawled. "I did not expect that. But you always had your head in a book. I can see writing as a natural progression."

Harbor laughed. "Honestly, I couldn't, but I love it. I get to help other people make their vision come to life. That's satisfying for me."

Ahmad took another step forward, so that there was no space between them. "And what is your vision, Tink? The one you have just for you."

Dear, Lord Jesus, is it hot in here, or is it just me? Please, don't let this man take one more step.

She shook her head. "In Atlanta, I knew exactly what I wanted and where I was going." Harbor looked at their intertwined hands. "Now, I'm not so sure."

Ahmad removed a free-flowing curl from Harbor's face. He leaned down to place a gentle kiss on her cheek. "Well, ma'am, I'm going to pray you find just what you want and just what you need." He grinned.

Harbor responded to Ahmad's smile with one of her own. "I appreciate that," she said. "What about you? Are you still working at your parent's store?"

Thinking about Honeybee Cards & Crafts, Ahmad's parent's chain of stores in the Hampton Roads Area, brought back fond memories for Harbor. Because Mr. and Mrs. Ferebee were not inclined to let Ahmad and Harbor hang out at their house without adult supervision, the couple made sure to provide a welcoming space for their son and his first love to hang out after school.

Harbor hadn't thought about those innocent, chill times with Ahmad in a while. The tender, long-ago memories sent the warm fuzzies to flight in Harbor's core, which she did not need. Ahmad's nearness was doing a stellar job of sending her emotions into overdrive all on its own.

"I should have stopped by while I was in town," Harbor continued.

"You are welcome to come to our old spot anytime. I think my mama and her new hip would do a backflip if you came walking through those doors."

The hearty laugh that shot through Harbor's core was real. She tapped Ahmad's chest. "Stop playing. I promise to stop by the store to say "Hey" on my way out of town on Monday.

Ahmad nodded. "Good, then you can see what I've done with the place."

"Do tell."

"Let's just say, as co-owner, I've made a few changes." He popped an imaginary collar on his navy tee shirt.

"Co-owner, Sir. Are you serious?" Harbor clasped her arms around Ahmad's waist. "Congratulations."

Ahmad's hands found their way to the small of Harbor's back. His chin rested on her head. "Thanks, Tink."

If not for hearing the clickety-clack of Patrice's chunky heels headed their way, Harbor would have lingered in Ahmad's arms until five minutes before the wedding, which was still two days away. At this point in the program, Harbor guessed she should extract herself from Ahmad's embrace, right?

She settled for taking in a soothing breath of his musky cologne. Harbor placed her hand in his. Being in Ahmad's presence again, with the air relatively clear between them, felt like life. She dared not put a question mark on this mini miracle.

They walked hand in hand through the living room to the foyer. Patrice looked at their linked hands and started to dance. "Okay, it is too late to make this a double wedding, but I am feeling the love, y'all."

"So extra," Harbor said, shaking her head. Her sister was as dramatic as they come. But she would be lying if she did not admit that walking away from Ahmad Ferebee again was not an option.

***

Harbor, a self-proclaimed realist, did not throw the term "magical" over a thing all willy-nilly. But seeing her sister and Colin exchange vows in front of forty or so witnesses at the lake was a magical moment no writer of a storybook tale could have improved on. Her mother had spared no expense in ensuring that the backyard affair flowed in flora from lily of the valley to white roses to Patrice's favorite flower...yellow and purple dahlias.

As Colin and Patrice stood inside the gazebo and were pronounced Mr. and Mrs. Colin Wilson-Banks for all the world to see, Harbor handed Patrice her bouquet of white and pink roses. She watched Colin thoroughly kiss his bride as the couple did "The Bump" off the gazebo steps to *Ain't No Stoppin' Us Now*.

Harbor spotted Ms. Amelia standing beside a distinguished-looking gentleman of a certain age, which she guessed to be somewhere in his late sixties or early seventies. The man wore a slick blue suit with a crisp white shirt accented by a blue and white polka-dotted bow tie. She watched in awe as the older couple began doing "The Bump" along with the other guests and the happy couple.

Get it, Ms. Amelia, Harbor thought and sighed with contentment. *This party is just getting started.*

The caterers unveiled a feast of what Patrice dubbed her bougie barbeque menu. Harbor sashayed through the onlookers toward her mother, ever the gracious host. Elizabeth mingled with guests, making polite conversation, and ensuring the caterers and photographer were on task.

Harbor walked up to Elizabeth and gave her mother a hug. Elizabeth leaned into the embrace for a long, precious moment, then stepped back.

"What was that for?"

Harbor grinned. "Because I love you, Mama, and I'm so glad I'm home."

"I'm so glad you are home too, my love," Elizabeth said, winking at her daughter. "More than you will ever know." At that moment, something caught Elizabeth's attention. She threw her hands up. "Oh, my goodness, why are they bringing out the cake now? It's not time."

Harbor turned around to witness two eager caterers walking out of the kitchen, holding the three-tiered dessert decorated with a rainbow of edible flowers. "You'd better get over there," Harbor said.

Elizabeth nodded. "I should." Before taking off in a mini sprint, Elizabeth grabbed Harbor's hand and squeezed. "Enjoy today. I'll talk to you later."

Harbor squeezed Elizabeth's hand and winked. "I will. Now go," she demanded.

Elizabeth did not need any further prompting. Her next target was clearly in her sights. She needed to keep the cake under wraps until it was time to unveil the lemon and French vanilla masterpiece.

When Patrice had summoned Harbor home for this surprise wedding, she could have never imagined she would not feel the heaviness she had held onto for a lifetime when all was said and done.

She prayed God would make all their next chapters much, much sweeter.

What was the scripture Ms. Amelia always quoted?

The verse floated to Harbor on the gentle breeze, gliding off the lake. The verse referenced God giving "a crown of beauty instead of ashes." Yes, that was what she needed. Harbor would willingly give God every bit of the ashes taking up space in her life for as much beauty as He wanted to send her way.

Harbor's gaze moved through the small crowd and landed on Ahmad. He stood by himself just at the edge of the lake. Although Harbor could not see his face, she knew something was off with him. Congregating with other people in a social setting was a part of Ahmad's love language. He blossomed in these types of settings, unlike Harbor. She could take and definitely leave all of the "How have you been" and "Let's catch up over coffee" small talk. What Harbor was becoming good at was talking to Ahmad. She missed just talking to her friend.

Harbor walked across the lawn to meet Ahmad, willing herself not to make a pit stop at the barbeque buffet. She was hungry and getting hangry. All her attention had been expended preparing Patrice for her big day, which included serving her baby sister breakfast in bed courtesy of Ms. Amelia. Harbor had swiped a maple link sausage from the plate of delights that had been lovingly prepared. That little piece of pork was long forgotten. She needed a plate filled with barbeque, potato salad, and a good-sized slice of wedding cake to make everything alright.

When she walked up to Ahmad, she could feel the tension radiating off him. The rumbles in her tummy would have to wait a bit longer. She slid her hand into his so that their fingers intertwined. Harbor wasn't even going to allow herself the space to analyze why she felt more than comfortable taking hand-holding liberties with this man like they were rolling up on their twentieth wedding anniversary.

She squeezed his hand. "You seem a little too glum for a man standing twenty feet away from what I have been told is the best barbeque in the State of Virginia."

He squeezed Harbor's hand. "Commonwealth, ma'am, please. You have been in Georgia too long."

Harbor laughed. "I guess I have. My apologies. Best barbeque in the *Commonwealth* of Virginia."

"Thank you."

A long silence found them staring out at the lake, looking for answers that were always out of reach.

"So, what's up, Mr. Ferebee?

Ahmad methodically rubbed his goatee. "Have you thought about what you will do after the wedding?"

Harbor wanted to laugh out loud at Ahmad's question, but she literally bit her tongue. Where she wanted to spend her time and who she wanted in her life were all she had thought about since coming home. Harbor knew without hesitation or doubt that she needed Ahmad Ferebee in her life. Period. She did not, however, know how many steps it would take for them to find their way to each other and never let go.

If he only knew.

"I fly back to Atlanta on Monday." Harbor could feel Ahmad's fingers become rigid with this revelation, but she needed to be honest.

"Where does that leave us?"

Harbor laid her head on Ahmad's shoulder. Where did that leave them?

"Well, Mr. Ferebee, I guess that leaves you in Virginia doing your thing and me in Atlanta doing my thing." It was a poor response, but what else could she say? They had not made any promises to each other.

"And us?"

Harbor let go of Ahmad's hand and leaned to embrace him. They stood in each other's arms for a long while before she spoke. "Maybe we can take some time to find our way back to each other. Become friends again."

Ahmad kissed Harbor's forehead. He inhaled deeply before saying, "I can work with that."

As the music played, laughter and the smell of barbeque floated around them, slowly dissolving the afternoon into the evening. Neither Harbor nor Ahmad planned to leave each other's embrace. Neither knew what the next minutes or moments would bring. But it didn't matter. Nothing mattered as long as they were a part of each other's lives again.

The End

A Place to Land

1

Elizabeth "Lizzie" Wilson had reached a crossroads in her life. At fifty-three, with a reasonable amount of life experience, she should have spotted the tractor-trailer-sized life events barreling toward her. But she didn't. Planning a wedding for her youngest daughter with a little less than a week's notice about the impending nuptials should have been the flashing neon sign her life was about to change.

Her baby girl, Patrice, had become the proud wife and self-proclaimed ride-or-die to Colin Banks four months ago on a gorgeous summer day in Elizabeth's backyard. She had no idea what a ride or die entailed, but Patrice was overjoyed with her decision. Her youngest daughter wanted nothing more than to spend all her remaining minutes and moments basking in the warmth of Colin's love. Elizabeth could admit there was nothing like young love, even if she was well past the happily ever after stage of life.

Less than a week after the "I do's," Patrice emptied her childhood bedroom of everything not affixed to the bones of the house and moved into Colin's end-unit townhome in Chesapeake, Virginia. In the past four months, Elizabeth and Patrice had only seen each other on the rare occasions when the newlyweds could spare an hour or two outside of each other's presence. And those occasions were getting more and more rare.

The anytime, anyplace mother-daughter bonding time she'd taken for granted was a thing of the past. With more than a bit of sadness, Elizabeth accepted that their Monday mall meet-ups and mani-pedi weekends were as dead as her car battery, she realized as she took another quick glance out her rearview mirror.

Elizabeth had broken down just outside of one of the library branches in Norfolk. She had planned to meet up with her oldest daughter, Harbor, for their version of girl-time, which was a lifetime in the making. Elizabeth had only recently begun to build an authentic relationship with Harbor after Patrice all but guilt-tripped them into planning her wedding and walking her down the aisle, mother on one arm and sister on the other.

After much prayer and time seeking God to understand why she had dropped the ball as a mother, Elizabeth realized building a healthy relationship with Harbor would require patience and love on both their parts. Meeting at the City of Norfolk's newest and truly grand library was a great start.

Harbor, a professional ghostwriter, used her gifts as a wordsmith to help up-and-coming authors who wanted their ideas to reach a worldwide audience. And she loved to visit libraries and soak up knowledge like a sponge, Elizabeth reflected as she watched a mother and her four or five-year-old daughter walk into the library. The little girl with the curly puffs, fire engine red rain boots, and pink tutu hopped and popped into the library. Elizabeth guessed the pair was headed to the children's section to get a seat for story time.

Elizabeth remembered how much joy Harbor had experienced at that same age when they'd made weekly visits to various libraries in the Hampton Roads Area. Their visits to the children's section would always conclude with a stop by one of the bakeries for a chocolate muffin and a container of chocolate milk. Elizabeth wondered if Harbor remembered any of the time they had spent just being a normal mother-daughter duo before she became an aloof and emotional sinkhole her daughter could not fill.

When Elizabeth glanced out her side-view mirror, she spotted Harbor's powder blue sedan turning the corner. She didn't understand why getting a glimpse of her oldest child caused her nerves to demand she acknowledge their existence. She and Harbor had spent time together at least a half dozen times in the last four months, just getting to know each other again. Elizabeth had even taken a trip to Atlanta to attend a book signing with one of the authors Harbor collaborated with. So why did she feel she was taking two giant steps backward instead of going forward into a bright, new chapter with her child?

Elizabeth knew she could not let fear settle in her spirit about her relationship with Harbor. By no means did she feel worthy of receiving her child's forgiveness. That being acknowledged, neither was she going to let the enemy guilt trip her into walking away from freely accepting Harbor's gift of mercy toward her.

"Father," Elizabeth uttered moments before Harbor pulled up beside her. "Help me to stand on your Word and to know who I am in you. Bless us, God. Thank you."

Elizabeth did not even attempt to explain the peace enveloping her as she rolled down her window just as Harbor pulled up.

Harbor turned on her blinkers and rolled down her passenger-side window. "Hey, Mom," she said. She glanced in her rear-view mirror to see a tow truck turning the corner. "Looks like I made it just in time. I'm going to park in the garage and meet you out front."

Elizabeth smiled at Harbor and probably stared at her for a second too long because her child gave her a quizzical look.

"Are you okay?" Harbor asked with genuine concern.

"Perfect," Elizabeth responded, grabbing her purse. "I'll see you soon."

Harbor nodded, then drove off.

Before stepping from her car, Elizabeth gave herself a cursory glance in her rear-view. Her fair complexion, dotted with freckles on her cheeks and the bridge of her nose, had only begun to show signs of aging. The fine lines appearing around her eyes should have sent Elizabeth into a frenzy and caused her to run to the nearest makeup counter to buy an overpriced eye cream to slow down the aging process.

I am not doing that. You are a beautiful woman of a certain age, she told herself. She gave her chin-length auburn bob a bit of a shake, then stepped out of the car.

The tow truck driver, a man that looked to be in his mid-fifties, wearing a faded blue jumpsuit, walked up to Elizabeth. He grinned, and Elizabeth was taken aback by the smile she saw radiating through his kind brown eyes. So, she smiled back.

"Thank you so much for coming," Elizabeth began, unsure what else to say. She handed him her keys.

She'd never called for a tow truck before. She'd had no reason to. Her husband had handled any car-related crisis...major or minor. When Bradford died five years ago, Elizabeth decided it would be easier to park her vehicles in the garage and secure a rideshare if she needed to go anywhere. She had only recently started to take her cars out for short trips around town to get comfortable with being behind the wheel again. It would have made sense for her to have one or both of her cars checked out by a mechanic before she hit the road in search of her newfound freedom. Hindsight was most definitely 20/20, she told herself.

"What is it that you need from me?" She asked, looking down the street, hoping she would see Harbor walking out of the parking garage.

The man smiled again and pulled out a card from his breast pocket. "My name is Mason...Mason Avery." He handed her his card.

Elizabeth accepted the card and gave it a quick glance. *Avery's Towing and Auto.*

"Thank you," she responded in a squeaky voice, like her vocal cords needed as much work as her car. And she was confident she knew more words than "Thank you." But what else could she say?

Mason seemed to sense her awkwardness and slid smoothly in for the save. "I believe you spoke with my daughter when you called. We have all your information on file and will give you a call when we figure out what happened with this beauty to make her interrupt your day." Mason tapped the roof of the rose gold SUV. "Did you need a ride somewhere?"

"Well, I," Elizabeth began to respond, stumbling over her words. *Pull yourself together.*

She noticed Harbor walking out of the parking garage and sighed with relief. She needed someone or something to save her from herself. Elizabeth pointed toward Harbor, who was moments away. "That's my daughter. We are headed to the library for a little girl time."

Too much information. Stop, please.

At that moment, Harbor stepped into the street to meet them. "Hello," she greeted. "Mom, are you ready? I am so excited to visit the library. And it's beautiful." Harbor gave the building, with its architectural flare, an admiring glance.

Mason nodded toward the library. "Is this your first time visiting?" He asked Harbor but looked at Elizabeth.

Elizabeth cleared her throat and responded to Mason's inquiry. "No, I've been here a few times, but this is the first time for my daughter, Harbor." She laughed nervously.

Harbor looked from her mother to the tow truck driver and then back to her mother. What in the world was she witnessing? Her mother's complexion was too fair to hide a blush. Was her mother blushing? Harbor took hold of Elizabeth's hand. "Mom, we should go in," Harbor said, guiding her mother toward the sidewalk. "But thank you for taking care of the car, Mr."

"Mason," he responded. "Mason Avery."

"Yes, thank you, Mr. Avery. Have a great day," Harbor said and simultaneously nudged her mother to awaken her out of this...she wasn't sure what state her mother was in.

Whatever was going on, Elizabeth finally figured out who she was and where she was, then said, "Yes, thank you, Mr. Avery."

"Please, call me Mason," Mason responded, preparing the car to attach to his tow truck.

"Yes, well, thank you, Mason," Elizabeth said before Harbor whisked her into the library.

Harbor was not trying to be rude, but she did not know how she felt about seeing her mother as a woman. Nah, she was not doing that today.

When they stepped inside the library, Harbor looked at her mother. "Are you okay?" She asked with more than a bit of knowing. "You seemed a little off balance." Harbor knew telling her mother she appeared to not be in complete control would get her attention, like nothing else. It did the trick.

Elizabeth put her purse in the crook of her arm, raised her chin, and looked Harbor in her beautiful almond-shaped eyes. "I am doing well, Love." She leaned over to give Harbor a hug. "Why don't we get this tour started," Elizabeth said, walking toward the stairs.

So, talking about the awkward flirtation with the tow truck guy was off the table, Harbor thought and laughed to herself. Since reconnecting four months ago, she and Elizabeth had run into all manner of unchartered territory. This was just another stop on their mother-daughter reconnect tour.

"I'm coming," Harbor responded, catching up to her mother.

***

Elizabeth could not have asked for a better day with Harbor. After leisurely perusing the library from top to bottom and participating in a meet and greet with several local authors from the Hampton Roads Area, they walked to Paxton Eatery for lunch. Because Harbor was still living in Atlanta and had not mentioned moving back to Norfolk, Elizabeth gave herself a mental pep talk to stay in the moment, during their time together.

They were seated at a table near a window, waiting for their server to bring their drinks. While they waited, Elizabeth prayed all would go well when she informed Harbor about an issue that had been pressing on her heart for several months.

Their server left their drinks and took their orders. Elizabeth wasn't all that hungry, so she'd ordered a grilled chicken salad with light balsamic vinaigrette. Harbor, never one to jump headfirst into a veggie lifestyle, ordered a cheeseburger with hickory-smoked bacon and fries. When their orders arrived, stealing a few fries was on Elizabeth's list of things to do. She couldn't go all in like her twenty-six-year-old daughter, but she would satisfy her taste for a little something fried whenever she could.

Harbor took a sip of her peach iced tea. "This is delicious," she said, watching the lunchtime crowd maneuver up and down the sidewalks, in and out of restaurants at lightning speed. A thirty-minute or even an hour lunch break only afforded a person a little time to truly enjoy a few moments away from work. Harbor was so thankful she worked in a career she loved, and that afforded her the space to live her life with a little more freedom than she may have otherwise had.

Writing for a living certainly presented challenges, but she loved her career. It didn't hurt that Harbor could pull out a pen and paper or whip out her laptop almost anywhere and anytime to jot down her ideas. The liberty of being a ghostwriter was one of the only reasons she could make so many trips back to Virginia to see her family.

Four months ago, no one could have told her she would be excited about returning to her childhood home to spend a few hours with her mother every other weekend. God had truly performed a miracle in all their lives.

Harbor placed her drink back on the table. "I need to slow down, or I won't have room for my cheeseburger. That would be tragic."

Elizabeth laughed and took a sip of her unsweetened tea. "No, that will not do at all," she said, dabbing at the corner of her mouth with a napkin. "Have you had a chance to see Ahmad already?"

Elizabeth knew asking about Harbor's first love would put her daughter in a good mood. Those two were meant to be. Elizabeth had always thought so, even if she did not always say so. For a long time, she had blamed herself for their breakup and canceled engagement. After Bradford died suddenly, Elizabeth had all but run Harbor away from home and away from the man that made her eyes dance, like they were doing now.

My baby is in love.

Elizabeth prayed Harbor and Ahmad would figure out what they wanted from each other and have the courage to be honest about their feelings. Since reconnecting four months ago, the couple made a grand show of making themselves and everyone else in their world believe they were just friends. Elizabeth did not have a friend in the world who could make her eyes sparkle like the night sky the way Harbor's did whenever she and Ahmad were in the same space.

Because Harbor was a grown woman with enough sense to make decisions for herself, Elizabeth decided to keep her thoughts about the matter under lock and key. She would gladly unlock the vault to have a little talk with Jesus about the matter, but that was as far as she was willing to go...for now.

When Harbor responded, she smiled. "No, I think we are meeting up tonight or tomorrow. Ahmad has been putting in a lot of late hours working with his mom and dad to restructure their company. Mr. and Mrs. Ferebee are considering selling at least two of their stores. They will still have the flagship store on Green Street, but Ahmad thinks they are ready to start a new chapter, you know. Have a little more freedom. Travel maybe. I guess I get that, but I can't believe they are really thinking about downsizing Honeybee Cards & Crafts."

Elizabeth could not have scripted a better opening for what she wanted to discuss with Harbor. She was ready, set, go to lay all her cards on the table when their server came over and, instead, placed their meals on the table. She and Harbor held hands and silently blessed their food.

They were only a few bites into their meal when Elizabeth said, "I wanted to run something by you."

Harbor stuffed a French fry in her mouth and mumbled, "I'm all ears. What's up?" She took a bite of her burger and then, as if remembering, put a few fries on her mother's plate. "Sorry, I almost forgot. You know how I am about potatoes."

Elizabeth ate several of the fries. "I vaguely recall," she responded mischievously. For the first few years of Harbor's life, all she could get her child to eat were mashed, baked, and fried potatoes as a side item with every meal.

My child...the potato fanatic.

She took a long sip of her tea, then said, "I wanted to know...." Just as Elizabeth was about to get this life-altering news off her chest, she looked toward the door to see someone near and dear to her heart walk into the restaurant. She hoped the new arrival could provide her with the backup she needed.

Francine Mills, her best friend, who she supposed was her ride-or-die, strode through the door in all her Afro-centric glory. Only Francine could rock a dashiki and leggings with as much style and flare as any twenty-something supermodel. Elizabeth's friend of nearly thirty years waltzed back into town several weeks ago after enjoying a six-month vacation, crisscrossing the globe post-retirement. Of all Elizabeth's "friends," most of whom quickly exited after Bradford's death, Francine proved to be a steady force that only God himself could separate her from.

Elizabeth watched as her friend inhaled an appreciative breath of the savory delights before heading over to their table. She stood to give Francine a warm hug.

"Thanks for meeting us."

"Oh, Honey," Francine crooned. "I would not miss this." She walked around the table to give Harbor a hug. "Hey, baby girl." Francine held her at arm's length. "From the look on your face, I have a feeling you had no idea I was coming."

Harbor shook her head and shot her mother a raised eyebrow.

"Not a clue, Auntie," Harbor confirmed, scooting herself and her food over to make room for Francine. She was always happy to see the woman she affectionately called "Auntie" even though the women occupying the table with her were not sisters.

It always amazed Harbor that even when her relationship with her mother was strained, which was most of the time before their reconciliation, she and Francine had always connected. They could talk about almost anything. The woman sitting beside her, smelling of raw-honey-based perfume, if Harbor had to guess, was truly her aunt. "But it's good to see you." She leaned over to give Francine another hug.

"Right back at you, Doll." She stole a fry and popped it in her mouth. Pointing a clear-coated, perfectly manicured nail at Elizabeth, she said, "Let's get this meeting started, shall we?"

Elizabeth rolled her eyes at her friend. She was starting to wonder if inviting Francine had been a wise move. What she wanted to talk to Harbor about would require a healthy dose of tact. It required knowing just what to say without saying too much. Lord knows she loved Francine, but her friend did not always know what to say, and she always said too much.

Help, Lord, Elizabeth prayed and made a mental note to connect with God on a regular basis...not just when she was in a desperate situation.

Well, here goes nothing.

2

Sitting beside Francine and across from her mother, Harbor felt like she was the hazelnut spread between two slices of honey wheat bread.

What are these two up to?

Harbor looked at her mother, who appeared nervous, folding and unfolding her paper napkin. She had not seen her mother this nervous since the super odd and super uncomfortable flirt session with the tow truck guy. Whatever Elizabeth had to say must be a doozy. Harbor pushed her plate to the center of the table. She was thankful she had eaten most of her food because her appetite was completely gone. It would have been an outright shame to waste all those fries.

Francine pulled Harbor's plate toward her and nibbled on the remaining fries. She looked from Elizabeth to Harbor and shook her head. "I have basket weaving at 5 and cake-decorating class at 7, so I'll start." She placed her hand on Harbor's arm. "Lovebug, your mama is thinking about selling the house."

"Francine!" Elizabeth blurted out. She scanned the restaurant to make sure she wasn't making a scene. No one seemed to hear her outburst, or they just did not care. "I would have liked to have given Harbor this news myself, *friend*." Elizabeth only pulled out the "friend" terminology when she was peeved. And right now, she was peeved.

"Well, *friend*," Francine countered, "you have been going back and forth about this for the last two months. It's exhausting. And as you well know, I spent half my vacation helping you develop a list of pros and cons about your next move."

Francine threw her head back in an ebullient laugh. She turned to Harbor. "Just imagine your auntie, sitting at a Parisian café, wearing a fabulous beret and sipping espresso while I discussed property values and other boring topics with your mama." Francine pointed to Elizabeth with a French fry like she held a medieval sword. "Not exactly how I'd planned on spending my time in the City of Light."

Elizabeth waved a dismissive hand. "Stop being so dramatic."

"Mom, are you really thinking about selling the house?" Harbor jumped in. She couldn't believe those words had even left her mouth. 137 Briarfield Lane was home. Never mind that she had cut off everything and anything to do with her childhood home for five years after her father's death. She was back now and regularly visited a couple of times a month. No, she wasn't ready to give that up. Harbor would never be prepared to give that up. "What about Ms. Amelia?"

At that line of attack, Elizabeth lost whatever steam she thought she had mustered. Ms. Amelia Livingston was their housekeeper, cook, friend, confidant, shoulder to cry on, and all the things she had never had in a mother or grandmother but had always wanted. Of course, Elizabeth was not about to put the seventy-something woman, no one knew her actual age, out of the house. If anything, she wished the mother-figure in their lives would consent to retire, so she could take care of *her* instead of the other way around.

Both Harbor and Francine stared at Elizabeth, anticipating what she would say next. Ms. Amelia was an integral part of each of their lives. Any decision Elizabeth made about the future would be made with the older woman's needs at the front of her mind.

"Harbor, I know this is unexpected," Elizabeth responded, hoping her words would assure Harbor that everything would work out just as it was supposed to. "But I haven't made any definite decisions. And whatever I do, Ms. Amelia will be well taken care of. That's not something you need to concern yourself with."

Harbor sat back in her seat and folded her arms across her chest. She stared at her mother, trying to figure out exactly what was going on. Why was she ready to pack up the house and move to where exactly? A condo? A retirement community for seniors? Elizabeth was only fifty-three. Did she even qualify as a senior? Harbor's head was spinning. She had too many questions and not enough answers. And to be clear, she was not feeling this motherly mid-life crisis.

"I don't understand," was all she could say.

Francine had her glossy, pink lips opened and poised to state Elizabeth's case for her, but she shot her best friend a warning look. She wanted and needed Francine's support, but she also wanted Harbor to understand her line of thought on this thing without the Francine spin. For once in their nearly thirty-year friendship, Francine "Franny" Mills shut her mouth and let Elizabeth take the lead.

Well, if anyone should take the lead on this thing, it should be me. I'm the one who is about to uproot her life for parts unknown...maybe.

Elizabeth reached across the table, palms up, and waited for Harbor to accept her hand. Her child sighed but complied. She gently squeezed Harbor's hand. Even the simple act of Elizabeth and her child holding hands was a victory in her world. She would take every win she could get. Mother and daughter may be on opposite ends of the spectrum about this move, but she could accept that for now.

"Nothing is set in stone just yet," Elizabeth began. "It's just something to consider. With Patrice living in Chesapeake with Colin and you in Atlanta, it's just me and Amelia in the house now. It really is too much space for just the two of us."

That was not new information, Harbor thought. They lived in a seven-bedroom mini mansion with more square footage than two or three families needed to live comfortably, but it was Harbor's home. It was home to all of them. Even when Harbor was doing her thing in Atlanta and pretending she did not want anything to do with her mother or anything taking place at 137 Briarfield Lane, she knew she could always come back. Where would she come back to if not home?

"What about the holidays?" Harbor asked. She knew she sounded like a little girl whose favorite toy was being donated to charity because of neglect. Was she neglectful? Probably. Harbor had a feeling she was serving up a heaping of "too little, too late," but she had to try. And nothing like a bit of guilt to get her to the finish line.

"Thanksgiving is just a few weeks away. And, I haven't been home in such a long time that I thought...." She let her words trail off. She knew she'd hit the intended target when her mother's eyes welled with tears. Gracious, she didn't want the woman to cry. Just not to sell the house. Francine pinched Harbor's thigh under the table. Yeah, she'd gone too far. "I'm just excited to come home for the holidays this year."

Elizabeth squeezed Harbor's hand and smiled. The tears that had threatened to fall only moments before seemed to retreat for now. "Are you really coming home for Thanksgiving?" Elizabeth asked and hoped she did not sound as needy as she felt. Harbor had not participated in their Thanksgiving celebration in a very, very long time.

Since reconciling, Elizabeth had hoped Harbor would come home to celebrate with her family and friends for Thanksgiving weekend. Still, she did not want to make assumptions. They were still in the midst of this healing journey, and she did not want to do anything to mess with their progress.

Harbor saw the anticipation dancing around her mother's eyes. "I will absolutely be there. I even plan on packing an extra pair of eatin' pants for Ms. Amelia's sweet potato jacks."

Both Elizabeth and Francine laughed and let out a collective breath. Harbor coming home for Thanksgiving was a big deal.

Francine nudged Harbor's shoulder. "Will a certain young man we all know and love be joining us?" She gave Elizabeth a conspiratorial wink. "There is always room for a little dark chocolate at our Thanksgiving table."

Harbor shook her head, feigning annoyance. "Yeah, that's a lot, Auntie."

Elizabeth snapped her fingers. "That is a great idea," she said. She pulled out her wallet and placed her credit card on the table. "Ladies, we are finished here." Elizabeth made certain her gaze locked on Harbor before she said, "I will get a ride home with Francine. I need you to invite Ahmad to Thanksgiving dinner."

"And his parents," Francine chimed in.

"Absolutely."

Harbor looked from Francine to Elizabeth. "Maybe it's just me, but I'm starting to feel like I don't have a say in this."

"You don't," Elizabeth and Francine said in unison.

Harbor rolled her eyes. *Great.* "Okay, I can do that," she said, leaning over in a loud whisper to Francine. "And while I'm taking care of that, maybe Mom can tell you about the very distinguished-looking tow truck driver that had her turning ten shades of pink. That should make for a fun conversation."

Francine leaned over the table, chin on folded hands. "Do tell."

Elizabeth narrowed her eyes at Harbor for a long moment, then allowed a slow smile to work its way to her lips. Without another word, she picked up her credit card and walked away to find their waitress.

Harbor laughed out loud. She stood, and Francine followed. "Don't let her get out of telling you."

"You know I won't." Francine laughed. "Just like I'm not going to let you get out of telling me what's up with you and Ahmad."

Not happening.

Harbor offered Francine a noncommittal smile and ran to catch up to her mother.

***

"Hey," Harbor said in a voice that sounded significantly more upbeat than she felt when Ahmad answered his phone.

"Hey, Tink. What's up?" Ahmad asked. Ever since he and Harbor had found their way back to each other, at least as friends, he had made it a habit of calling Harbor by the nickname he'd given her in high school. Ahmad could not say definitively why he started calling Harbor "Tink," but the endearment seemed to fit, and she'd never objected. "I thought we were meeting for dinner later tonight. My mom and I are making progress with everything at the store, but it's taking a little more of my time than I thought it would." He laughed. "Scratch that, a lot more of my time."

Harbor rubbed the back of her neck. She could feel the tension from the day mounting. She wasn't sure why she was trippin' about her mother possibly selling the house. But she was. Saying goodbye to her childhood home was not on her list of things to do when she'd hopped in her car and gotten on the road from Atlanta.

"Tink, you okay?" Ahmad asked.

"Guess what?"

"What?" His response was deliberately slow.

"I'm outside."

"What...woman." Ahmad hung up the phone. He walked out of his parent's cozy cards and crafts shop to see Harbor's car parked in the very last parking space near the front entrance.

By the time he'd walked over to the car, Harbor stood by her door, wearing a sheepish look. Maybe sheepish wasn't the right word, he decided. The look on that beautiful, espresso-brown face with the dimple taking center stage on her left cheek definitely looked much more like premeditation. She was up to something.

Before Ahmad went in for the question-and-answer period about this impromptu visit, he gathered Harbor in a hug. He missed this woman. Their nightly video chats did not make up for his longing to be in her presence. Ahmad let the embrace linger before he asked, "So, what's up? I thought we were meeting at the oceanfront."

"Oh, we are definitely going. You are not getting out of taking me for a delightful seafood dinner," Harbor responded, stepping just out of his embrace. This man smelled too good and looked too fine for her to casually linger in his embrace like they were the couple they had once been.

No, she and Ahmad were just friends. At least, that was the line she had been feeding herself for the last four months. But the look of desire radiating through his beautiful brown eyes was telling her something completely different. Yeah, they needed a little more space. Harbor took a step back and bumped into her car door.

Ahmad touched her arm. "Careful," he said with a grin.

"I'm good. And I know you have a lot going on with the store. I don't want Mama Ferebee giving me the business about keeping you from the business." Harbor laugh-snorted at her own joke.

Ahmad shook his head. His ebony locs swayed with the motion. "Please, I have made peace with the fact that my mama likes you a little more than she likes me. I have no idea why because I'm an amazing person. But it is what it is."

Harbor dusted imaginary dust off the shoulder of her army-style jacket. "Favor ain't never been fair." Even after she'd skipped town five years ago without a word to anyone about her whereabouts except for Patrice, Ahmad's mother had made a point of keeping in contact with her. Mama Ferebee would text Harbor a word or two of encouragement each week just to let her should-have-been daughter-in-law know she was loved and would be welcomed back into their family with open arms. No, favor was not fair, but she thanked God for it every day. "I think Mama Ferebee is pretty great too."

Ahmad rolled his eyes. "You and Mama can schedule a who-loves-whom-more session some other time."

Harbor stuck out her tongue. "We will."

"Good," Ahmad said and stuck out his tongue in response. "I thought you were hanging out with your mom at the library today. Did your plans change?" He asked tentatively.

When Harbor had come back into town for Patrice's surprise wedding, Elizabeth had crushed Harbor's tender spirits by not showing up for an appointment with her at his cousin Kelsey's boutique for a pre-wedding shopping trip. When Elizabeth and Harbor finally talked about the incident, Elizabeth admitted she had intentionally missed the appointment because she wanted to give her daughter and Ahmad the time they needed to reconnect.

Since Elizabeth felt responsible for their breakup, she also felt responsible for giving them every opportunity to reconnect. Ahmad wasn't sure how well Ms. Elizabeth's plan had worked because he had been parked in the friend zone with Harbor for the last four months.

Be patient. She is worth waiting for.

At the moment, his mental pep talk was not helping him. Ahmad was grateful when Harbor interrupted his thoughts with a play-by-play of her day.

"No, we met at the library," Harbor began. "And it was amazing. But that's not why I'm here." Harbor folded her arms across her chest and let out a long-suffering sigh. "At lunch today, Mom told me she's thinking about selling the house. Well, Aunt Francine showed up, and she was the one that spilled the beans. But can you believe that she wants to sell the house? It's a family house. Who sells a family house?"

Harbor inhaled sharply then continued. "And I can't even get into my mama flirting with the tow truck guy. I mean, he was cute for an older dude, but really. Isn't there some unwritten rule that mothers don't flirt with possible significant others in front of their daughters? It was off-putting."

Ahmad looked a little too serious when he asked, "So, you thought the tow truck guy was cute?"

Harbor playfully tapped his shoulder. "Shut up. Did you even hear my whole selling-the-house rant? She's thinking about selling our house."

Ahmad placed her hand in his. His voice was low when he asked, "You think maybe she needs a change?"

"A change." Harbor huffed and leaned against the car door. "Elizabeth "Lizzie" Wilson is a woman of leisure. She's never had to work to earn a living. She does what she wants to, how she wants to, and when she wants to. Her life is already her own. What more could she want?"

Ahmad walked over to stand beside Harbor. He nudged her shoulder. "You should talk to your mom. See where her head is with all this."

Ahmad knew his suggestion was walking a fine line between always having Harbor's back and taking Elizabeth's side. He glanced at Harbor briefly and could see this news had shaken her up. Elizabeth deciding to move on with her life seemed like a healthy and necessary move to Ahmad, but Harbor was obviously not feeling it. He just couldn't understand why.

Harbor had not lived in her childhood home for nearly six years since she broke off their engagement and left town. Ahmad wondered why she wanted to hold on to a place she'd all but written off. He was about to say as much when Harbor flipped the script with an unexpected request. Revealing whatever insight he thought he had into the situation would have to wait.

Harbor turned to face him. "I'll take talking to my mother about the house under advisement," she said.

"Got it," he responded, taking a step forward. Ahmad knew he should retreat, but he had no intention of doing so. If Harbor was not feeling him the way he was feeling her, the only person he would harm was himself. Being this close to Harbor, looking into the deepest parts of her soul through her warm, brown eyes did not feel like it was hurting him. It just felt right.

When Ahmad closed the space separating them, Harbor knew she should jump into her car and get out of there any way she could. She and Ahmad were friends. But was a friend supposed to feel fireworks jumping off in their tummy when the "friend" in question invaded her personal space? "Um...so, here's the deal," Harbor began, not liking how her voice sounded unsteady and unsure. This was Ahmad, for goodness' sake. Whatever feelings they had for each other couldn't just be resurrected...*could it*?

Harbor decided she needed to make her request and do it with a quickness. She needed to get out of there. Summoning her composure, she said, "Mom wanted me to invite you and your parents to Thanksgiving at our house."

Ahmad smiled that wide, disarming grin. He slid his hand into hers so that their fingers intertwined. Ahmad leaned into her ear and whispered, "We accept."

Harbor's internal alarm screamed for her to back up.

Friends don't kiss friends if they want to remain just friends.

Instead of giving her trusty alarm the time of day, Harbor allowed herself to gaze into those mesmerizing eyes. She allowed herself to look at him, and all she wanted at that moment was for Mr. Ahmad Ferebee to kiss her fully and completely. Oh, how she missed his kisses. Harbor placed her hands on his shoulders and herself on the tips of her fire engine red sneakers with every intention of kissing that man. When Ahmad put his hands around the small of her back, she knew they were taking a step that could not be undone.

As Ahmad leaned into kiss Harbor, they were both jolted out of the moment by the rhythmic sound of the chime as the door of Honeybee Cards & Crafts opened. They released each other like two five-year-old cookie thieves with their hands caught in the cookie jar. Before either of them could stumble through an awkward I-have-no-idea-what-just-happened explanation, they were greeted by the ear-to-ear grin of Ahmad's mother, Cherice Ferebee.

The petite woman, rocking a mini afro with golden tips, wearing a blinged-out dungaree and a string of pearls, gave her son a knowing smile before she embraced Harbor. When Cherice released the woman she hoped would be her daughter-in-law, she told Harbor, "Sweetie, I have missed you. It's been too long."

Ahmad sighed and rolled his eyes. "Here we go with the love fest. It's only been a month since Tink came down for a visit." Even as he admonished his mother for making a fuss over Harbor, he couldn't help but agree that it had been too long since they'd seen her – since he'd seen her.

Cherice tapped Ahmad lightly on his shoulder. "Like I said, it has been too long. I missed my sweet girl."

Harbor gave Cherice another hug and made a face at Ahmad. When the two women released from their embrace, she said, "I missed you too, Mama Ferebee."

"How long are you in town for, Love?"

"Just through church and brunch on Sunday afternoon, then I head back to Atlanta."

It wasn't lost on Ahmad that Harbor did not describe her trip back to Atlanta as going home. Maybe she was a little more tied to Norfolk than she let on, but he could never be sure with Harbor. Even when they were in a committed relationship and months away from becoming man and wife, there was still a hidden area of Harbor's heart that Ahmad did not have access to. Maybe that would change with time and a little more patience on his part.

"Well, don't wait another four weeks before you come to visit. I would love to come down to see you in Atlanta," Cherice pointed to the store. "But this place has us running a little ragged, trying to do inventory, consolidate merchandise, blah, blah, blah." She laughed. "I said all that to say that I love to see that smiling face."

In response, Harbor offered Cherice a wide grin. "Well, if you accept my invitation to come to Thanksgiving dinner, it will only be another three weeks before we see each other."

"Done!" Cherice beamed. "I don't have to cook, and I get to spend Thanksgiving with my best girl. That is a win for me."

Ahmad winked at Harbor. "See, I told you we accept."

Cherice placed her arm around her son's waist. "We absolutely accept."

"Perfect. Mom and Aunt Francine will be two happy women."

"No happier than me." Cherice laughed. "I haven't eaten a Thanksgiving meal I haven't prepared myself since Ahmad was born. I would say I am long overdue for a beautifully prepared meal."

"Agreed," Harbor and Ahmad said in unison.

Cherice laughed. "You two are always on the same page. It's so sweet."

Mama Ferebee and her hyper-optimistic assessment, Harbor thought. Neither she nor Ahmad responded to the observation. Harbor had sense enough to know they may be on the same page, but they were absolutely on different plot points. Heck, if she and Ahmad could find their way to the same paragraph, that would be a win in Harbor's book.

Ahmad was ready to move forward as if they had not had a five-year gulf between them. Harbor, well, she was content just to have him in her life again. It was just that simple.

Harbor opened her car door and leaned in to give Cherice a hug. "Well, I need to go home for a bit."

"Safe travels, Sweetie," Cherice finally said, walking back toward the sidewalk, leaving Harbor and her son to themselves.

When Harbor was in her seat, she looked up at Ahmad and asked, "Are we still meeting up tonight, Mr. Ferebee?"

Ahmad looked at her for a long moment before he said, "Absolutely."

"Good," Harbor responded. She closed her door, waved, then drove off. Apparently, neither of them could put together more than a word or two without it being awkward since their "moment" several minutes earlier. She hoped their dinner tonight would not be weird.

Ahmad stood beside his mother on the sidewalk and watched Harbor drive away. He released a resigned sigh. "Ma, I'm not sure how long I can do this."

Cherice cocked her head. "Do what, Son?" She asked. "Wait for the woman you love to come back to you?"

"Exactly."

"Well," Cherice said, walking back toward the store. "I guess you need to ask yourself if Harbor is worth waiting for."

Ahmad did not miss a beat when he responded, "She is."

Cherice opened the door, then turned around before she said, "Then wait."

3

When Elizabeth asked Francine to give her a ride home, she had neglected to calculate how long it would take for her friend to pummel her with questions about Mason, the tow truck guy, and their conversation with Harbor about selling the house. She and Francine had been parked in her driveway for the last forty minutes, going over a play-by-play of the day from the time she'd handed over her car keys to Mason.

Between Francine's endless questions and subsequent advice, Elizabeth would glance out her window at her two-story brick home with ivy vines snaking their way to the balcony of her second-floor bedroom. Her home really was beautiful and a sight to behold. So, why was she thinking about walking away from the home she'd lived in, loved in, laughed in, and maybe even despised from time to time for the last thirty years?

For what seemed like the hundredth time to Elizabeth, Francine asked, "So this tow truck guy was cute, wasn't he? If he wasn't, I doubt you would have turned 'ten shades of pink' like Harbor so eloquently stated."

Elizabeth turned to face her friend. She did not miss the look of longing in Francine's magnificently wide grey eyes. Her sister-friend was lonely and had been for a very long time. For anyone who dared to look beyond the self-assured façade Francine wore like a well-tailored suit, they would know her friend desperately wanted what she never had...a family of her own to love and dote on. With all the uncertainty and challenges in her life, Elizabeth knew she was blessed. She would do well to remember that from time to time.

"Honestly, I wouldn't say he was cute," Elizabeth began. Francine was nearly at the edge of her seat, waiting for more details. Watching her friend bounce in her seat with schoolgirl anticipation tickled Elizabeth. "I would say he was average," she said.

If Francine's jaw could have hit the floor, it would have at that moment. She gave the steering wheel a whack with her hand. "That's unfortunate. I was looking forward to living vicariously through you with tow truck guy. Oh well. Maybe your water heater will go, and tow truck guy's cute cousin will show up to save the day."

Elizabeth couldn't help but laugh. "I don't need a water heater fiasco to find a man. Thank you very much. And you, my friend, are too amazing to waste your time living vicariously through me."

Francine rolled her eyes and started the engine.

"So, I guess we're done," Elizabeth stated matter-of-factly. She opened the door and stepped out of the car. "And by the way, tow truck guy was not cute or average. The man is gorgeous. A salt and pepper goatee graced the smoothest caramel complexion I have seen in a very long time."

"Ooh, I knew it," Francine all but screamed. She shut off the engine and hopped from the car. She ran around to meet Elizabeth and hooked arms with her friend. "Basket weaving can wait. I need all the details. Spare nothing."

The two women walked up the drive toward the front door. Elizabeth allowed herself to be guided by Francine up the steps. At the door, she turned to her friend. "What am I doing?"

Francine did not miss a beat. "Finally starting to live. And it's about time." She laughed, following Elizabeth into the house.

***

Elizabeth and Francine sat on the sofa in the parlor. Francine reached for another of Ms. Amelia's unreasonably delicious oatmeal raisin cookies. She took a long, indulgent bite of the chewy delicacy. "If I didn't know any better, I would think Amelia is purposefully siding with the enemy in my battle with the bulge." She slid the plate toward Elizabeth, who was sipping a cup of lavender tea. "You know I'll finish them off if you don't save me from myself."

Elizabeth laughed and placed the plate on an end table. She knew how much her friend loved anything Amelia's seasoned culinary hands crafted. "Happy?" She asked, placing her cup on the table.

Francine tossed the last bit of the cookie in her mouth. "No, but I'll survive." She scooted near Elizabeth so that their knees nearly touched. "So, tell me all about this new romantic interest."

Elizabeth started to object, but Francine continued, "And we need a new name for him besides tow truck guy. He is a grown man. And what are we...fifteen?"

Elizabeth shook her head and sighed. "His name is Mason Avery. And...."

Francine's eyes widened. She grabbed Elizabeth's arm. "Wait...Mason Avery? The Mason Avery that owns at least 20 auto repair shops up and down the East Coast? *The* Mason Avery that donated $20,000 to several local charities? The Mason Avery that was named one of Norfolk's most eligible bachelors for the last three years? That Mason Avery? Oh, Honey, you picked a winner."

Elizabeth wondered if her friend could say the man's name just one more time, she inwardly laughed. She hadn't seen Francine this excited about anything since she'd won concert tickets from her favorite radio station last fall. Apparently, seeing several of her favorite bands from the nineties did not compare with the man of the hour...Mr. Mason Avery.

Elizabeth took a long, excruciatingly slow sip of her tea before she responded, "I guess that's him."

Jumping from the couch, Francine did her solo version of the samba around the room. When she finally stopped and allowed herself time to catch her breath, she exclaimed, "My friend, you have reeled in one of the most eligible bachelors in the state!"

Elizabeth threw up her hands. "Pause. I haven't reeled in anybody. The man is fixing my car, Franny. It's as simple as that."

"Yeah, right," Francine responded, taking her seat. "You forget, I know you. I know what interest in a man looks like in those eyes of yours. I haven't seen that spark since the day you met Bradford Wilson at Harbor Love Stadium. I know that look, Lizzie Wilson."

At the sound of her husband's name, Elizabeth felt the burgeoning emotions of the present colliding unceremoniously with the complicated feelings of her past. She was a widow and had been for five years. But did that give her a right to just move on with her life? *This is crazy.*

She stood, but Francine touched her arm gently, halting her retreat. Elizabeth looked at Francine and willed herself not to release the tears that wanted to flow. She had always prided herself on being able to control her emotions. After reconnecting with Harbor and releasing her emotional healing to God, all that changed. She was in touch with her emotional self in a way she had never been. The process of healing old wounds frightened her, but she refused to run away from the process. There was healing in each step.

Elizabeth did not try to stop this latest wellspring. "Franny, this is a lot," she barely croaked out as the tears flowed. "What is wrong with me?"

Francine grasped both of Elizabeth's trembling hands. "Nothing is wrong with you, my friend. This is what we call being ready to move on with your life." She squeezed her friend's hands. "And I am so happy for you."

Grabbing a napkin from the table and dabbing her tears, Elizabeth laughed. "Bradford would throw a fit if he knew I was even thinking about moving on."

"Oh, I know. I loved Bradford like a brother, but that man was a jealous mess when it came to you."

Elizabeth nodded vigorously. "Yes, he was, especially at the beginning of our marriage. But he got better, thank God. You remember I was five seconds from leaving him when we found out Patrice was on the way. I don't know if he got a Holy Ghost warning or what, but he eventually got his mind right."

Francine shrugged. "Maybe it was the Holy Ghost. Maybe it was him coming home to an empty house the night you decided to leave. Whatever happened, Bradford figured out what he needed to do, and he did it."

"Thank God he did."

Francine stood, pulling Elizabeth up with her. "And even if he didn't, Bradford is gone. His cold, dead hands can't stop you from being wooed by another man."

"Francine!"

"I'm just saying." Francine picked up her purse and walked toward the door. Elizabeth followed. "Stay open."

Before responding, Elizabeth made sure that their gazes connected. "You too, my friend."

Francine winked. "You always did give good advice."

Shaking her head, Elizabeth laughed and watched her friend walk to her car.

4

Stupid unresolved feelings.
Harbor could kick herself. And she so deserved a good, swift kick in the rear for not guarding her heart around Ahmad. Didn't having on the full armor of God include being protected from emotional angst brought on by oneself, she reasoned. *Okay, maybe not.* What made her think she could waltz into town, almost kiss the man she used to call her fiancé, and not be called out on the carpet?

In a twist Harbor did not see coming, it wasn't Ahmad who was pressuring her to "Reel that fish in or cut the line." No, the unsolicited decision-making strongarming was coming from the 110-pound bulldozer parked beside her on the pew at Shelton Avenue Church of God in Christ.

To anyone that did a surface-level assessment of Harbor's baby sister, Patrice, they would see a fresh-faced twenty-five-year-old newlywed. Her sister had the beauty, grace, and intelligence to obtain everything the world had to offer.

All Harbor could see at that moment was the five-year-old version of her annoying little sister, even as Patrice and her husband Colin joyfully participated in praise and worship. Harbor usually loved visiting Shelton Avenue. It was a relatively small congregation of worshipers with only one hundred or so members. But the Word Pastor Ramsey delivered every Sunday, along with the melodic sounds of the choir and praise team, fed Harbor's soul with enough meat to satisfy her until she could visit again. Not this Sunday.

The only thing Harbor was being fed was heaping servings of Patrice's advice to "Get your mess straight with Ahmad and do it soon." Harbor recalled her conversation with Patrice after leaving Ahmad's at his parent's store on Friday. She was so conflicted about what nearly happened with Ahmad that she needed to talk to someone before she imploded. Patrice was usually her very willing, very patient sounding board about all things Ahmad Ferebee.

Apparently, things had changed since Patrice added the till-death-do-we-part hyphen to her last name. Harbor watched Patrice and Colin stand in unison as the praise team rolled into their rendition of *This is Freedom*. The song usually made Harbor stand up and get her praise on, but not today.

Today she was too busy thinking about Patrice's annoying yet completely relevant advice about her love life. Not to mention that Ahmad was singing in the choir, looking with complete admiration at a gorgeous diva who was belting out her favorite song. This was definitely not her day. The faster she could make tracks back to Atlanta, the better.

Despite herself, Harbor found her foot tapping to a performance that she could only describe as fire. When Patrice leaned over and hit her arm a little too hard, Harbor winced.

"Girl, get up," Patrice yelled as the soloist and choir repeated the song's catchy hook.

Harbor mouthed, "Pass."

Patrice hunched her shoulders and continued to get her praise on. After she and Colin sang the last view bars of the song with the choir, Patrice sat down and nudged Harbor's shoulder. Patrice's eyes darted toward the soloist, who stepped back to take the empty seat beside Ahmad. She looked back toward her sister. The soloist leaned over to give Ahmad a hug that lasted a little longer than it should have and was a bit too friendly.

"She's not the only one," Patrice advised.

At that ominous prediction, Harbor quickly scanned the choir stand. Two men in their late fifties or early sixties were sprinkled among twenty or so women in every age range. Harbor noticed a few women flinging darts, with their eyes, at the overly friendly soloist.

Looks like she wasn't the only contender for Ahmad Ferebee's heart. The difference between Harbor and his jealous singing buddies was their complicated history.

Harbor realized as annoying as her baby sister could be at times, Patrice was right about one thing. All her back and forth with Ahmad about them being just friends was about to pop her in the face like a pie gag on one of those old-school, black-and-white television shows.

Time to reel that man in or cut the line.

***

After the service, Harbor stayed glued to her seat and watched as Ahmad made his way around the lingering congregation to greet many of the other worshipers. Close to his heels was the beautiful soloist, seeming to hang on to Ahmad's every word. Each time Harbor had visited the church, she had never noticed the woman with the melodic voice that was making her feel some kind of way.

"Girl, fix your face," Patrice demanded when she walked back over to Harbor after making small talk with a few other members. She wedged her narrow frame between Harbor and the end of the pew. "All that mean-mugging is unnecessary. If you want to be with the man, just say so. Trust, Ahmad will shoo away his little groupie in a heartbeat."

"What's her name?" Harbor asked and made a conscious effort to fix her face. "I'll bet it's Tammie. The cute ones are always Tammie, Sammie, or some kind of Ammie."

"Her name is Kelly, and you sound crazy."

Harbor groaned. "Don't you think I know that?" She forced herself to stop watching Ahmad and Kelly's tour around the church and turned to face Patrice. "Will you talk me into doing what I know

I need to do but am too scared to do on the way to brunch," she begged. "Please!"

Patrice stood. Harbor followed her lead. "No can do." She stepped out of the pew. "I'm exhausted and not feeling a big meal today. And my hubby is pressed to get home to watch football. I think he's already in the car, so I'm about to head out."

Harbor laid a hand on Patrice's arm. "Something's not right with you. You don't care one thing about Colin watching football. We are Bradford Wilson's girls. Basketball all the way. So, what's up?"

"Look, Sis, I'll talk to you later." That was all Patrice could get out before the two women were greeted by Ahmad and Kelly, still clad in their Kente cloth choir robes.

Ahmad gave Patrice a quick side hug and made a beeline for Harbor. "What's up, Tink?"

Harbor leaned into his embrace, closed her eyes, and enveloped his spicy cologne.

Lord knows this man should not smell this good.

When she opened her eyes, she was greeted by Choir Kelly's perfectly arched raised eyebrow and a disapproving, thin-lipped grimace.

Harbor stepped out of his embrace. "Hey," was all she could say in response to *her* ex-fiancé. Looking into that flawlessly beautiful yet intensely evil glare coming from Choir Kelly was getting to her.

Ahmad smiled. "If you don't have plans for lunch, you should come to Mama Honey's Grill with Kelly, me, and a few of the other members. You know you love their biscuits."

Harbor had to laugh at that. She loved anybody's biscuits. Mama Honey, Aunt Honey, Papa Honey, whoever. She almost accepted his invitation, but one look from Choir Kelly and her appetite was gone.

"Maybe next time. I have a date with my mom for brunch." Harbor thought she spied a look of disappointment on Ahmad's face, but she couldn't be sure.

Harbor held out her hand toward the other woman. "Hi, I'm Harbor. And you have a beautiful voice."

Kelly slowly extended her hand toward Harbor. "I've been told."

Oops, time to go.

Harbor wanted to run to the ladies' room to scrub the stank off her hand, but she was her mother's child. Her manners would not take a backseat because this chick was trippin'.

"Okay, nice to meet you, Kelly." She turned to face Ahmad. "I'm heading back home tonight. I'll call you when I get there."

"How about you call me when you get on the road. We can talk while you drive. Can't have you falling asleep."

Harbor did not have to look at Kelly to know that Ms. Beauty Queen was sporting a nasty scowl. She gave Ahmad another quick hug. "It's a deal."

"Bet." Ahmad turned to leave with his sidekick nearly glued to his side.

Patrice and Harbor watched the pair walk out of the church. "See what I mean? Either make your move soon or forfeit the game."

Harbor groaned. "I hear you, Sis." She looped her hand through Patrice's arm as they walked out of the door. "Loud and clear."

***

If Harbor had known having brunch with her mom would feel more like a college study session instead of another dose of mother-daughter bonding time, she would have taken Ahmad up on his offer to join him and his fellow songbirds for lunch. Yeah, that was not going to happen. Little Ms. Attitude made sure of that.

Harbor had never been a brawler, but it was something about Kelly that made her want to summon her inner boxer and suit up for a bit of one-on-one in the boxing ring. Wow, was she really thinking about fighting over Ahmad? She had to get a grip on this thing. Fighting over a man was not her jam. Harbor also decided she needed to get a hold of this depressing lunch date with her mom.

When Harbor reached across the dining room table to grab another biscuit from the basket, Elizabeth beat her to the punch and passed her the basket. Harbor took a biscuit and placed it on her plate. "Thanks," she said in a voice that sounded a little too forced and a little too upbeat.

"Absolutely, my love." Elizabeth took a sip of her iced tea. She smiled.

Harbor smiled back. She loved when her mother called her "my love." It always gave her heart something she didn't know it was missing. Having the opportunity to return to Briarfield Lane at her leisure and have Sunday brunch with her mother was part of why she was hesitant about the house being sold.

Time to look this elephant square in the face, Harbor decided. She took one last bite of her almond-crusted herb salmon and dove into what was in her heart.

"Mom, are you really thinking about selling the house?"

Elizabeth wiped her mouth with a linen napkin and placed it on the table. She looked around her dining room at all the treasures she had gathered over the years. Most were classic pieces that included several Nigerian and Cameroonian paintings that were a nod to her ancestry she wanted to leave to her girls. The rest of the seven-bedroom house had much of the same feel. 137 Briarfield Lane had encompassed everything in her world for over thirty years.

Elizabeth locked eyes with the beautiful child she loved so much and thanked God every day was back in her life. "It's something I've considered."

"But," Harbor prodded.

Elizabeth extended her hand across the table. Harbor accepted her mother's hand. "I want to do the right thing for you and Patrice. I know this house means a lot to both of you. And I don't want to snatch it away from either of you."

For the first time, Harbor could really see her mother. She could see the struggle Elizabeth was going through. She wasn't a mother yet, so maybe she could not fully understand the sacrifices parents made for their kids...even their grown kids who would be rolling into their thirties in no time. She respected her mother even more for considering how she and Patrice would feel about not having this space to come back to.

Harbor squeezed her mother's hand. "Have you talked to Patrice yet?"

Elizabeth twisted her lips. "I tried speaking with Patrice yesterday, but something is going on with that girl. And I don't think it's just that she's a newlywed either." She took another long sip of her tea, thinking. Elizabeth's next words were low when she said, "I think your baby sister is pregnant."

Harbor held on to her chair with both hands and shimmied around in her seat. "That makes so much sense. When I talked to her after church, she said she was too tired to come for brunch. And said that she wasn't really hungry."

"Patrice hasn't been tired since the day she was born, and she is always hungry."

"Always," Harbor agreed. "Aw, a baby. You think she even knows?"

Elizabeth nodded. "I think she does. Not sure if she's told Colin yet. I think she's nervous about something going wrong. And I completely understand. I didn't have any peace until I held you and Patrice in my arms. I couldn't shake the feeling something would go wrong." She sighed. "At some point, God gave me a revelation that changed everything."

Harbor narrowed her eyes. "What's that?"

Elizabeth said thoughtfully, "God is in charge of every part of my life, including the lives I had growing in me."

"That is really beautiful." Harbor smiled. She loved this version of her mother. "We'll pray that Patrice finds that peace too." She grabbed another biscuit from the basket and stood. She took a bite. "I thought Ms. Amelia was having brunch with us today after church."

Elizabeth stood. She ran her hands down the front of her lavender and cream pantsuit to smooth out any wrinkles. "It's the pastor's anniversary at her church."

"Let me guess. Ms. Amelia wanted to make a statement with one of the new hats you bought her for her birthday last month."

Elizabeth pointed to Harbor. "She did, indeed. Amelia pranced out of here, wearing a pink and green polka-dotted suit and matching hat."

Harbor threw her head back and laughed out loud. "That woman loves her sorority!"

"Yes, she does." Elizabeth walked around the table and enveloped Harbor in a loving hug. "When are you headed back to Atlanta, my love?"

Harbor lingered in her mother's embrace. "I wanted to leave tonight. I think I'll get a good night's rest and head out in the morning."

"I love having you in the house with me. So that sounds good."

Harbor walked with Elizabeth toward the staircase. "I forgot to ask, when do you pick up your car?" Her gaze held a knowing glint when she looked at her mother.

"Tomorrow, and that is all I have to say about that." Elizabeth started to walk up the steps. She stopped beneath a picture of Bradford. She lingered for a long moment, trying to find something in her husband's gaze that gave her something she needed from him to move forward with her life.

Harbor seemed to sense her mother's plight. "Mom," she began. She waited for Elizabeth to face her. "Whatever you do about the house and the really handsome man at the auto shop, Patrice and I will be fine. We're good."

Elizabeth smiled at her child and released tears she did not know she was holding onto. She gave a last look at Bradford's picture and walked up the stairs. "Thank you, Baby," she called back to Harbor.

***

The only thing Harbor wanted to do was to see Ahmad's beautifully stubbled face before she went to bed. Talking to Ahmad, even for a moment, would ensure she had a great night's rest before she hit the road at 6 a.m. for what she was hoping would be a smooth ride to Atlanta.

Sitting on her bed with her laptop, Harbor ran a hand through her twist out to ensure her hair had just the right bounce before she called Ahmad. She knew she needed to calm down. This was Ahmad, for goodness' sake. He never looked at Harbor with anything but pure joy, whether she was wearing a bonnet and a tattered robe or a form-fitting evening gown with stilettos.

Harbor didn't want to wait until tomorrow to call Ahmad. She wouldn't be back in Norfolk for another three weeks and wanted to tell him everything. She needed to express all her feelings once and for all. Harbor had a feeling if she waited any longer to make this love connection, Choir Kelly would be all too happy to swoop in with a sexy siren's call. She could not let that happen.

And if this all played out the way Harbor hoped it would, Ahmad may decide to make a trip down to Atlanta for a little visit.

She held on to Theodore Goodnight, a snuggly little gift from Ms. Amelia on her fifteenth birthday. She kissed her furry companion's cheek before sending Ahmad a video call.

Ahmad picked up his phone on the second ring. He offered Harbor a slow grin, and his smile definitely reached his eyes. "Hey, Tink."

"Hey," Harbor said, not meaning for her greeting to come out all breathy, but that was just the effect this man had on her. *Bring it in, girl.* "How are you?"

"Good," He drew out the word. "And I'm guessing you are not in your car headed to Atlanta since you are all snuggled up with Mr. Goodnight."

Harbor smiled. "You would be correct. I decided I would stand a better chance of not falling asleep on the road if I got a good night's rest. Thought I'd be benevolent and not inflict harm on my fellow travelers."

Ahmad laughed. "Wise choice," he responded, fingering the stubble on his chin. "If I had known you were staying tonight, I would have dropped by. I could have beat you in a game of cards and kept up my winning streak." He counted on his fingers. "What are we like thirty games to zip?"

Harbor tossed a stray twist behind her ear. "Whatever, Sir. A comeback is imminent. Prepare yourself." She laughed. "And besides, I thought you were hanging out with your girl, Kelly."

Ahmad stared at the screen for a long moment before he asked, "What's up with all that?"

"What's up with what," Harbor asked, feigning innocence.

"You, Tink. You sound like you got something to say. And Kelly is not my girl. So why do you sound jealous?"

"First, I'm not jealous. Second, why would I have anything to say about you and Kelly? I don't even know her. Literally just met her today."

"First, there is no me and Kelly. Kelly is my friend. Like you and I are just *friends*, right? That's what you said we were."

This conversation was going left fast. "Of course, we are friends, Ahmad. We've always been friends since I had braces, and you thought you were going to become the next great basketball star."

But we finally grew up, and now I want more. I want us to be what we were before I walked away.

Harbor wanted to scream those words, but nothing came out except her lame, "We've always been friends," nonsense. "I love being your friend, Ahmad."

Did it again.

Ahmad's relaxed features went rigid at Harbor's declaration. "Tink, I'm going to say goodnight. You have a long drive tomorrow and need to get some sleep."

Harbor threw her hands up. Theodore Goodnight flew across the room and landed on his head near the door. "What is wrong with you? We just started talking. Why are you acting like this?"

"Because I'm tired." He sighed.

"Then get some sleep, Grumpy. I'll call you tomorrow after I get home."

"I'm not sleepy, Tink," Ahmad said and paused for what seemed like an eternity. He knew he should probably end the call before he said something he could not take back. But his fragile heart was not listening to his spirit man. "I think we need to take a step back." The words were out of his mouth before his always-at-the-ready filter could sift through his anxious words.

Harbor shook her head. "I...I don't understand." This was not happening.

What is happening?

"I need some time. And I think you do too."

"Time for what?"

"To figure out if I am what you want. If I'm the man you want to be with. Because I can't do this version of friends with you anymore. It's too hard."

Harbor released a laugh that lacked mirth. "Are you really giving me an ultimatum?"

Ahmad pinched his lips and said, "Yes, I am. Goodnight, Tink."

Harbor did not know how long she stared at her laptop's screen after Ahmad ended their conversation. This could not be happening. Why couldn't she tell Ahmad she loved him? Five years ago, she'd walked away from Ahmad without looking back. She didn't respond to a text, answer his phone calls, or even send a forwarding address. Was this her punishment for walking away? Harbor didn't believe in Karma, but this felt like payback.

Ms. Amelia would tell Harbor she needed "a good long meeting with Jesus" more than she needed to understand why her plans to tell Ahmad she was ready to be with him ran into a brick wall.

"God, please help," was the last thing Harbor remembered saying before she fell into a fitful sleep.

5

Elizabeth woke up bright and early Monday morning. She'd hoped to see Harbor before she got on the road to Atlanta, but her oldest child must have left the house well before sunrise. Elizabeth received a text just before 6 a.m. from Harbor that she expected to be in Atlanta by three.

She would give her a call later to make sure all was well. At the moment, she needed to find her way to the kitchen before Ms. Amelia could begin her usual breakfast preparation. Elizabeth wanted to give her longtime cook and friend a special surprise, something that the older woman would not see coming and hopefully would not turn down.

For the next hour, Elizabeth worked on her breakfast preparation. A hazelnut and maple coffee blend happily percolated in the coffee pot. A ham and mushroom quiche was ready to come out of the oven. The cranberry muffins she'd picked up from the bakery needed a quick zip in the microwave. Breakfast would soon be served.

Just as Elizabeth had taken the quiche out of the oven and placed the cheesy delight on the marble island, Amelia walked sleepily into the kitchen.

The older woman looked from the quiche to the coffee pot, then to Elizabeth, who grinned sheepishly. "Girly, what are you doing?" Amelia walked over to the quiche, sniffed, and nodded approvingly.

Elizabeth cut servings of the quiche and placed each slice on plates with a fruit medley and muffins with honey butter. "What does it look like I'm doing?" She asked, walking the plates to the table. After bringing the coffee pot to the table, she took a seat and eyed Amelia. "You plan on letting my food get cold?"

Amelia shook her head and quickly strode over to the table. "Well, I reckon not." She held out her aging hands to Elizabeth. "Lord, I thank you for this day. And I thank you for this meal. It looks good and smells right nice. Let's just hope it tastes like something. Amen."

When Elizabeth opened her eyes, she smirked at her longtime friend. "Hush and eat."

For a long while, the two women ate in silence. After a few bites of quiche, Amelia slowly nodded and chewed with satisfaction.

That was all the thanks Elizabeth needed. She knew Amelia was the real cook in this family. She was just happy to serve her up something that gave her joy. Elizabeth hoped her next surprise would be taken with just as much acceptance.

After taking one last bite of honeydew melon, Elizabeth pushed her plate aside. "I have one more surprise for you."

Amelia raised her chin. "What you up to, Girl?" She asked suspiciously.

"Doing something I should have done a long time ago." Elizabeth reached across the table to grasp one of Amelia's hands. "Amelia Marie Livingston, you have been like a mother to me and my girls. We love you so much. You have taken care of us through every storm, wind, and rain."

Amelia shook her head. "I didn't wake up this morning with no plan to cry, and here you go, making me cry." A single tear slipped down her cheek. "You know I love my girls."

"I do," Elizabeth responded and gently squeezed Amelia's hand. "And that is why I say with all the love in this life and the next, you, Ms. Amelia Livingston, are fired."

Amelia's mouth flew open, but not a single word came out. When she finally got her bearings, she said, "Excuse me, little girl. Have you lost your natural mind?"

Elizabeth threw her head back in the loudest, most unencumbered laugh she had remembered having in years. She stood, pulling Amelia up with her. Elizabeth gave her friend a quick hug. "I said what I said. You are fired from your role as the housekeeper of 137 Briarfield Lane, but your role in this family is forever."

Amelia visibly relaxed.

"You already know I have set up a retirement account for you that is ready to be used anytime you are ready to tap into it."

Amelia opened her mouth to speak, but Elizabeth kept going.

"You were supposed to retire just before Bradford passed away, but you waited because you wanted to make sure I would be okay. Then you pushed off retiring again because you wanted to make sure Patrice had everything she needed." Elizabeth swiped at a stray tear.

She continued, "Then you wanted to be here when Harbor came back home. Well, Patrice has everything she needs in Colin, and we have our Harbor again. It's time for you to focus on you. And that is why I have set up for you a ten-day stay at a luxury resort in New York City. While you are there, you can visit your sister, Janice, and her kids. They haven't seen you in a while. And I know they miss you."

Amelia was speechless. Amelia Marie Livingston was never speechless. What was she going to do with all this attention? All this time on her hands? Well, God had given her the Wilson family to fill up her days for nearly thirty years, and she loved every minute of it. She reckoned God knew how to fill up the rest of her days.

"Well," Amelia began with a bit of a haughty tone. "I guess I am officially a lady of leisure."

Elizabeth laughed and hugged Amelia again. "Well, I guess you are." She began to clear the breakfast dishes. "I am going to take care of these, and then I need to call a ride so I can go pick up my car."

Amelia huffed. "You going to get that car and maybe something else, I been told."

Elizabeth scraped the leftovers off the plate into the garbage disposal and placed them in the dishwasher. "I see Francine has been running her mouth."

"All day, every day." Amelia laughed. "I am going to do something I haven't done in much too long."

Elizabeth gave her friend a quizzical look.

"Honey, I'm getting back in the bed."

Elizabeth smiled as she watched Amelia walk out of the kitchen. There was a lightness in her step that was beautiful to witness.

***

Elizabeth sat in the back of the rideshare she'd ordered as the car drove down Toliver Street toward Avery's Towing and Auto. She didn't know why she was suddenly getting so jumpy. She needed something to occupy her thoughts.

She considered engaging her driver in conversation but thought better when she noticed an "Out to Lunch" sign dangling from one of his vents. Elizabeth couldn't say what was in her driver's thoughts when he put up the sign, but she decided to err on the side of caution and let him concentrate on getting her to her destination.

A safe bet would be to give Francine a call. Her longtime friend was always ready and willing to engage in conversation. Elizabeth wasn't surprised when Francine picked up on the first ring.

"Hello, my friend," Francine crooned into the receiver.

"Hello to you too." Elizabeth laughed. "You must have that phone glued to your hip. I have never known anyone to answer a phone so quickly."

Francine huffed. "I happen to be waiting for a very important call this morning." She let her words hang in the air like freshly washed clothes hanging on a backyard line.

"Since I know you weren't expecting a call from me, I'm curious who this mystery caller is."

Francine paused for a long moment. "Promise you won't go all mama bear on me."

"No promises, Franny. Spill it."

"Well, lately, I've been thinking about my life and what I want to do next. These last few months of retirement after working five days a week as a school counselor have been...."

"Boring," Elizabeth finished her thoughts.

"Yes, and you know me. Doing nothing is not what I'm about doing. The vacation was great, but it wasn't enough. And all these classes I'm signed up for are starting to get on my nerves. If one more person in that basket weaving class tells me I may want to think about signing up for a different class, I think I might scream."

Elizabeth had to laugh. She had no idea why her friend even signed up for basket weaving. The woman was not artsy, and she certainly was not craftsy.

She looked at the GPS on her driver's dashboard and realized she had another fifteen minutes or so to go before reaching the shop. In that time, she should be able to get Francine to spill her guts and tell her friend a bit of what was in her own heart.

"So, basket weaving isn't going great. I won't even get into the fact that I told you it wasn't the hobby for you," Elizabeth stated.

"Please don't," Francine requested. "Basket weaving aside, I've decided what I want to do with the next part of my journey."

"I would love to hear."

"I think God has put on my heart to look into becoming a foster parent. Is that crazy at my age? I mean, fifty-three and becoming a parent for the first time. Who does that?"

"Oh, Sweetie, that is not crazy at all. You are going to make an amazing foster mother or adoptive mother if that's what you decide to do. And you know that what looks crazy is sometimes exactly what God wants us to do."

"You are right about that, my sister," Francine agreed. "Thank you for always having my back."

"It is my pleasure. Are you expecting a call from the agency this morning?"

Francine giggled. "I should find out by noon today."

"I'm so excited. I am praying for you, my friend." Elizabeth paused for a long moment before she said, "And when you get a minute, pray I don't make a complete fool of myself when I pick up my car."

"What time are you going?"

"Now," Elizabeth responded, taking another peek at the GPS. "Well, I should be there in about five minutes."

"What's to be nervous about? You are just picking up your car, right?"

Elizabeth sighed. "Unless you talk me off this ledge, I thought I might invite Mason to Thanksgiving dinner. Is that crazy? That's crazy."

"No, Honey. That's you taking the bull by the horns. I am so here for this. You got this."

"Franny, my palms are sweating."

"What are you wearing?"

"Dark denim jeans, a white top with a black cardigan, and black boots. Why?"

"Great. I just wanted to make sure you wouldn't have embarrassing pit stains. Run your hands down the front of your jeans a few times. That fabric is thick enough to soak up the moisture without leaving a stain."

"And that's why I love you."

The car pulled into a parking spot in front of the garage.

"Franny, I have to go. I'm here."

"You got this, Girl!"

Elizabeth released a long sigh to expel the mounting tension in her neck as she opened the car door. "Let's hope so." She disconnected the call and thanked the driver before closing the door.

***

Elizabeth stood at the front desk of the auto shop. She hadn't spent much time in auto shops since Bradford had handled all things car-related during their marriage, but this one looked pretty nice from what she could see. The front desk was all business, with a sleek black phone, a laptop, and a tiny bell for customers. There was a magazine rack in the corner and several cushioned seats beside a table, holding hot coffee and snacks.

If Elizabeth wasn't so nervous about meeting Mason again, she would make herself comfortable and have a cup of coffee while she waited. She knew the bell was there for her convenience, but she always felt like she was being extra even when she needed assistance. And she had only been waiting a few minutes. No big deal.

Elizabeth was just about to walk over to the magazine rack to occupy her time for a bit when she looked up to see Mason coming into the shop from another door behind the counter. She was greeted by his welcoming, bright smile.

Mason walked around the counter to greet her. He extended his hand and immediately withdrew it. "I'm so sorry. I haven't had a chance to wash my hands. I was just finishing up with your car."

Elizabeth smiled and waved off his concern. "It's no worry at all. I'm just glad you could work on it over the weekend and have it ready for me today."

Mason spritzed several pumps of hand sanitizer on his callused hands. "Believe me, it was a joy to work on your car. And it was an easy fix."

"Easy?"

"Just needed a battery and an oil change. Have it serviced regularly, and you should be in good shape."

"That is good to hear," Elizabeth responded in a voice that she hoped sounded confident but also thankful for his help. She looked at his hands and noticed he was holding her keys. This transaction would be over in no time.

Chickening out of her self-imposed crisis was becoming a viable option. The longer she stood there talking about car stuff, which she was not really interested in, the greater the chance she would take her keys and head down the road and not look back.

Don't be a coward, Lizzie.

She was about to do just that when Mason's next words stopped her in her tracks. "If you are not in a rush, would you like a cup of coffee?"

Elizabeth released a breath. "I would. Thank you."

They walked over to the little table. Mason pulled out her chair, and she took a seat. He poured them both a cup of coffee and added cream and sugar to his cup.

Elizabeth added sugar to her coffee and prayed she would think of something to say to this man. Between sips of coffee, she thoroughly looked at the man across from her. She realized why Mason Avery was considered one of Virginia's most eligible bachelors. He was a handsome man if she ever saw one. The blue jumpsuit he was sporting couldn't hide his muscular physique. Not bad for a man who was probably in his mid-fifties.

"Ms. Wilson."

Elizabeth heard her name being called, but it felt like the voice was blowing in on a spring breeze. Nice and gentle.

"Ms. Wilson."

This time, Elizabeth heard her name loud and clear. She was staring at the man's chest and hadn't heard a word he'd said. She took a sip of coffee to cover her embarrassment.

Get it together, Lizzie. You are an adult. Focus.

"I'm so sorry. I've had an eventful morning. My mind was somewhere else."

Mason took a long sip of his coffee. "Believe me, I understand."

Elizabeth offered a slight grin. She was thankful he hadn't called her out on her long, drawn-out perusal of his distinguished-looking self. She decided that women taking a second or third look at him was probably nothing new since he was labeled a "good catch."

Whatever that means.

"We're busy all year long," Mason continued. "But the holidays are especially busy. I usually get here around seven and work through lunch. This is a nice break."

Elizabeth nodded. She stood, realizing she was probably taking up a lot of his time. Mason Avery seemed to be a self-made man, and time was money. "This has been nice, but I should let you get back to work."

The disappointment in Mason's voice was evident when he slowly stood and said, "I appreciate your time and business, Ms. Wilson."

Elizabeth waved him off. "Please, call me Lizzie."

So apparently, I am good to go with a relative stranger calling me by my nickname.

Well, one bold step deserved another. "Mason, I was wondering if you have plans for Thanksgiving. I know it's only three weeks away, but...."

Mason's gracious smile had returned. "My daughter, Kenya, is going out of town this year to meet her fiancé's parents. So, I'd planned to pick up a turkey sandwich, watch a few games, and call it a day."

Elizabeth was shaking her head vigorously at those words. She knew she could make him a better offer. "Would you like to have dinner with me and my family? It's a small group. Just nine of us if you don't mind downhome food, lots of conversation, and the best roasted turkey you have probably ever eaten...guaranteed. And because you don't know us, I will also guarantee that my crew is on their best behavior." She laughed.

Mason clapped his hands. "I believe I would be a fool to turn down an offer like that," he said, handing Elizabeth her keys. "And I am no fool." He held on to her hand for a moment, then walked toward the door.

As they walked out of the building, she called off her cellphone number. Elizabeth was about to walk around the building to pick up her car when she stopped in her tracks. "Oh, my goodness, Mason. I am so sorry, I forgot to pay my bill." Elizabeth began to fish through her purse for her credit card.

Mason placed a gentle hand on her wrist.

Elizabeth stopped and looked into his eyes. Those pools of milk chocolate were mesmerizing. She needed a good talk with Jesus to stop her from diving into all that beauty...at least for now.

"If that Thanksgiving meal is as good as you promised, I will be paid in full."

Elizabeth smiled. "You won't be disappointed."

"I don't believe I will be."

6

Harbor could not believe it had been over two weeks since she'd driven back to Atlanta. When she'd finally made it home after ten long hours of driving in bumper-to-bumper traffic, she purposely threw herself back into the grind of working twelve-hour days. Thinking about her jacked-up attempt to tell Ahmad she was ready to start anew was not up for discussion.

Harbor realized after playing the 1990's hit, *Love Takes Time,* on repeat that the song chronicling the murky path of love was quickly becoming her unofficial anthem. Because the song was taking her to a place she could not easily crawl out of emotionally, she decided to let the heart-wrenching melody play out for a final time before she turned the volume down on her phone.

In Harbor's ever-increasing world of drama, maybe love took exactly five years of nothing, four months of back and forth, and an act of God to bring something resembling a lasting happily ever after to fruition.

Maybe an act of God was what it would take to bridge the impasse Harbor and Ahmad were facing. In the last two weeks, neither she nor Ahmad had made a move to contact each other. The only reason Harbor could safely say the man was still alive was that Patrice had not blown up her phone with a "911," signaling something tragic had happened. No, Ahmad Ferebee was not injured or about to take his last breath; he was just ghosting her.

Harbor opened her laptop and decided the only way she would get through this day without sulking in the sting of rejection was to get back to work. She opened a file titled *Ida B. Wells and the Fight.* Her editor, Clarissa Barrett, had sent her the shell of a manuscript from a woman who wanted to author a series of short stories about the tenacious investigative journalist and her fight to expose lynchings occurring throughout the South in the early 1900s.

Because Harbor was a self-proclaimed history nerd and sponge for anything remotely related to the African American experience, she immediately responded to Clarissa's email that she would take on the assignment.

Usually, when Harbor began a new writing assignment, the blank page staring at her was a challenge she was ready and willing to conquer. It was her version of David slaying Goliath with a few smooth stones and a lot of God on his side. However, after opening the document for a tenth time and seeing nothing more than an italicized title staring back at her, Harbor knew she needed a little help.

Her editor, as cool as she appeared on a surface level, would pop her top if Harbor did not submit the first draft of a fifty-page short story the day before Thanksgiving. At 4'11, sporting a blonde pixie cut and usually wearing overalls, most people assumed Clarissa would take anything thrown her way. That was not the case. Harbor had seen more than one of her colleagues given a dressing down for not living up to Clarissa's high standards.

Harbor could not go out like that. She could admit to being many things...stubborn, impetuous, and even willful at times. A character trait she would never ascribe to herself was being a flake. Harbor had not missed an assignment since signing on with Clarissa five years ago. Heck, she'd never turned in a late assignment. Not even in high school or college. Harbor did not plan on becoming someone who could not be depended on to keep her word.

Harbor pushed her laptop aside and picked up her phone. Opening her contacts, her fingers automatically scrolled to Ahmad's name. He was always her first choice. *Always*. Not today. They were on the outs, and she needed to talk to someone who wouldn't pull punches. Patrice to the rescue.

Her baby sis picked up on something like the tenth ring. Yes, Harbor was that desperate. Hanging up was not an option.

"Hel...hel...hello," Patrice finally said.

"You sound crazy. What's wrong with you?"

Patrice made a nasty sound like she was about to throw up in her mouth. If Harbor had assessed the situation correctly, she probably already had.

"Sis, are you at home?"

"Home...um, does the bathroom toilet count?"

"Oh, my baby. Okay, I am sending you a grocery order with a boatload of ginger chews, ginger ale, salted crackers, and chicken soup. I heard all that is supposed to help with morning sickness. Not sure about the chicken soup, but it's chicken soup. Can't go wrong."

Patrice made another retching sound. "How did you know? Colin! He told Ahmad, and Ahmad told you. He is a dead man. So dead!"

"Calm down, crazy. Ahmad and I haven't talked since I came back to Atlanta. So, you can call off the hit on Colin. Mom and I figured out I'm going to be an auntie about two weeks ago," Harbor said in a singsong melody. "I'll text you when the groceries are on the way and call you back later."

"Okay, thank you. I'll take the groceries but don't hang up. Why'd you call?"

"It's nothing," Harbor lied.

"You never call me when you are supposed to be at that laptop, typing away." Patrice sounded just a little better.

Harbor hesitated. "I have this project that's due right before I hit the road to come home for Thanksgiving, and I still don't know what to do about Ahmad."

Patrice's one-word solution simultaneously annoyed and calmed Harbor.

"Pray."

"Pray?"

"Yes, be real with God, and He will be just as real with you," Patrice said before she made another retching sound. "Love you, Sis. Thanks for the groceries."

And with those parting words, Patrice was offline, and Harbor was left to do something she had neglected to do since coming back to Atlanta...pray.

***

For reasons Harbor could not explain, the thought of approaching God about her relationship with Ahmad gave her an uneasy feeling. How could she confide in God about such a trivial matter? In her head, she knew God was in charge of all things and wanted to be a part of every fiber of her life. Even when she and her mother were on the outs, she always prayed her family would be safe and protected, and no harm would come to them. She prayed the same for Ahmad and his family.

Harbor could never find the right words to ask God about her relationship with Ahmad. Because this thing with Ahmad felt like a boulder, pressing unapologetically on her chest, maybe God did not view Harbor's love drama as trivial.

She found a comfy spot on her honey-brown leather couch and opened her bible app. Since the one thing she knew she needed more than anything at this moment was wisdom, she opened Proverbs. Harbor didn't know where this search would lead, but she hoped it would give her just what she needed.

Lord, I need your help. Please and thank you.

As Harbor ended her very abbreviated prayer, the proverb she landed on after a random scroll was Proverbs 3 verses 5-6: *Trust in the Lord with all your heart and lean not on your own understanding; in all your ways submit to him, and he will make your paths straight.* The one area in life Harbor had become a pro at was leaning heavily on her own way of doing things. She let her own thoughts figure out the who, what, when, and where each and every time before going to God if she went to God at all.

Trust seemed like such an easy concept, but nothing was easy about taking a matter out of her hands and placing it in God's. When she was the one in charge, Harbor could at least have a say in the outcome. Trusting God with her life evoked a visceral reaction in Harbor's core that terrified her. Maybe after doing things her own way all this time, Harbor could trust in something greater than herself.

Instead of jumping back into her work, Harbor chose to sit, meditate, and just listen. And taking a few deep breaths would not hurt anything. Maybe if she stopped running, she could finally hear God speak. Perhaps *He* wanted to be a God in her life that she sought more than on Sundays after breakfast and before brunch. That was something Harbor had never considered before.

Well, God, if you want to speak to me about Ahmad or anything else in my life, I am listening.

7

Elizabeth realized Thanksgiving Day would not be the relaxed family event she had envisioned as soon as Harbor showed up at six o'clock that morning and made a beeline for her room. Harbor had been locked away in her childhood bedroom for nearly three hours. Not even the delightful smell of Ms. Amelia's honey butter biscuits coming straight out of the oven had caused her to venture out of her space.

Because Elizabeth exercised the right every mother did from time to time to unashamedly get in their child's business, she tapped on Harbor's door as she held a tray with hot biscuits and a cup of cinnamon cocoa. She was not above a little bribe. But she refrained from leaning into the door to listen in on whatever was or was not happening in there. Harbor was a grown woman and deserved space to figure her life out without motherly intervention.

And Elizabeth would give her eldest all the space she needed to do her own thing as soon as she looked into those lovely brown eyes to ensure all was well. "Harbor, sweetheart. How are you doing?" Elizabeth heard Harbor jump off the bed and run to the door.

Harbor swung the door open and graced Elizabeth with a smile she would never grow tired of seeing. At least Elizabeth hoped the smile radiating on Harbor's face was for her, not the biscuits. Who was she kidding? *It's definitely the biscuits*, Elizabeth laughed inwardly.

"For you." Elizabeth handed Harbor the tray.

Harbor inhaled the scent of biscuits and hot cocoa like she'd just stepped through the gates of heaven. She accepted the tray and danced to her bed, which looked like a paper factory had exploded over the pastel patchwork quilt. Even her beloved teddy bear, Mr. Goodnight, was barely visible beneath a mound of scattered papers.

Harbor placed the tray on a nightstand, then shoved the offending papers to the foot of her bed.

"Thank you for this," Harbor said, grabbing the tray and flopping onto the bed. "We can share."

Elizabeth did not immediately move. She savored the sight of watching Harbor dancing back and forth as the sensation of the biscuits and warm honey hit her tongue, sending her child's taste buds into an otherworldly experience. Elizabeth was thankful to watch Harbor take delight in the small things. The small things mattered.

Elizabeth walked over to the bed and made herself comfortable. She grabbed a plush pillow and placed it against the headboard. Her lower back needed all the stability it could get. She grabbed a biscuit. "Don't mind if I do."

Harbor laughed. "And if you didn't, it would be gone in a minute."

"Believe me, I know."

They ate in companionable silence, enjoying their impromptu breakfast for several minutes before Elizabeth spoke. "I was wondering what had you trapped in this room on Thanksgiving," she began, picking up one of the many papers scattered about the bed. "Please don't tell me your boss expects you to work today."

"No, this is all me." Harbor took a sip of her cocoa. "This is delicious." She placed the cup and tray back on the nightstand. "I can't seem to stop writing. It's like something is pushing me forward. Yesterday, I turned in the first draft of a story I'm developing. All these other ideas started coming to me about the next installments on the drive home. Apparently, driving alone in a car for nine hours straight is the perfect way to get my creative juices flowing." Harbor laughed.

Elizabeth listened with fascination as Harbor talked about the short stories she was developing. She wouldn't take credit for Harbor's love of writing. The gift of taking words and fitting them together like an intricate puzzle was God's special anointing he'd bestowed on Harbor to use in her own unique way. Elizabeth only hoped their trips to the children's reading room at the library when Harbor was a child played a small part in the beautiful gift she was developing one word at a time.

She placed her hand over Harbor's hand. "I am so proud of you, my love. But don't stay in this room all day." Elizabeth stood. "Get those ideas out and come downstairs. You know Amelia does not want us fooling around in her kitchen, especially on Thanksgiving. But I think she would appreciate our company."

Harbor squeezed her mother's hand. "Will do. What time are you expecting everyone to arrive?"

Elizabeth stood and walked over to the other side of the bed. She picked up the tray. "Around four. Ahmad and his parents are still coming, correct?"

Harbor grimaced and shrugged.

"You want to talk about it?"

Harbor shook her head so vigorously that the pen she'd tucked behind her ear flew out. "Not really." She hastened to add, "But I have prayed about it."

Elizabeth leaned over to brush a delicate kiss on Harbor's cheek. "My love, that is the best thing you could have done." She walked toward the door. Turning, Elizabeth said, "Now, pull yourself together. I will not have you looking a mess when our company arrives."

Harbor narrowed her eyes. "Company? My baby sister, her hubby, and Auntie Francine are not company. They've all seen me in sweats and a tee."

"But Mr. Mason Avery has not. And he will not see you looking less than your best today." Elizabeth winked at Harbor and made her way down the hall as fast as her heeled slippers would take her.

Aw, my mommy has a man friend.

***

To Harbor's surprise, Ms. Amelia "allowed" her and Elizabeth to help prepare the meal. Truth be told, they were relegated to salad and iced tea duties, two relatively safe tasks. Aside from the menial nature of the tasks, Harbor counted working alongside Ms. Amelia and her mother for the first time as a win.

Harbor jumped when Ms. Amelia swatted her behind with a kitchen towel after she mistakenly used grape tomatoes for the salad instead of cherry tomatoes. If there was a difference between the two varieties, Harbor had never noticed or cared. In Harbor's estimation, heirloom, grape, cherry, beefsteak, or any of the thousands of other varieties of the fruit masquerading as a vegetable each served the same delicious purpose.

For the sake of keeping the peace in Ms. Amelia's domain, Harbor obediently remade the salad, using organically grown cherry tomatoes if the labeling on the package was accurate. She would do just about anything for the woman who loved her with as much compassion and grace as any "grandmother" could. Her mother and father's parents died before Harbor's fifth birthday, so she could not even claim fleeting memories of being loved and adored by her nana or papa.

Harbor watched Ms. Amelia joyfully scurrying around the kitchen. The head "chef" tested the thickness and flavor of the gravy, cut corn off the cob for sweet cornbread dressing, and zested lemons for the tangiest and sweetest lemon bars ever to grace a Thanksgiving table. At twenty-six, Harbor felt exhausted watching the seventy-something woman bounce from one task to the next like an exuberant teenager with boundless energy. Harbor thanked God that He saw fit to send her family a treasure in such a loving, selfless person as Ms. Amelia Livingston.

Ms. Amelia walked up behind Harbor and wrapped her in an embrace. "I am so glad you are home, baby girl. You have no idea."

Harbor hugged Ms. Amelia in return, then shooed her away. The loneliness of every Thanksgiving she'd spent in Atlanta away from her family begged to find a release. The determined pool of tears welling in her eyes could not be kept at bay for much longer. "I am too. More than I can say. But I promised myself no crying today. So, you need to keep it moving, Missy, before my mascara blazes a mucky puddle down my cheeks. Please and thank you."

Ms. Amelia leaned in for one last squeeze. "Well, we can't have that."

Elizabeth chimed in. "No, we cannot. You two can get as sentimental as you want after we eat."

Just as Harbor swatted at a tear, sliding down her cheek, the doorbell rang. She covered the salad with plastic wrap, tore off her apron, and ran to the front door. She heard her mother and Ms. Amelia warn her to "slow down."

Harbor hoped Patrice and Colin were the first to arrive. She needed to lay eyes on her baby sister to ensure the life growing in Patrice's womb was cooperating with their mama. Not that she could do anything to lessen Patrice's bout with morning sickness.

Harbor was experiencing her own bout of big sister guilt. She had spent nearly every moment of the last few days seeking God's direction about her relationship with Ahmad and racing to complete her project at work just before the deadline. The toilet-gate incident had long been forgotten, along with the random, daily text she usually sent Patrice.

Harbor did not bother peeking at herself in the mirror before answering the door. Both Patrice and Colin had witnessed her looking her best and looking a mess. So, no biggie.

When Harbor opened the door, "No biggie" quickly turned into "No!" Why were Ahmad and his parents standing at her door, dressed to the nines in their holiday best and grinning like they anticipated a Thanksgiving feast? Harbor had not talked to Ahmad in three weeks. A full three weeks! Maybe she was trippin', but zero communication signaled to Harbor that a happy Thanksgiving meal was not in the cards for them.

"I'm guessing the look of confusion on your gorgeous face is confirmation that Ahmad did not call to tell you we were still coming," Cherice said as she stepped forward to hug Harbor. She stepped back to stand between her son and husband.

"No, ma'am, he did not."

Both Cherice and Harbor shot Ahmad the look.

Ahmad shot back with an apologetic smile to his mother and a quick "my bad" shrug to Harbor.

Cherice tapped Ahmad's shoulder. "I told you to call Harbor to confirm." She shook her head with as much disapproval as a mother could throw at her adult child. Cherice held her hand out to Harbor. When Harbor reached for her hand, Cherice said, "Sweet girl, I am so sorry we rolled up on you like a bunch of rogue holiday party crashers. But I don't think I have it in me to leave after smelling whatever Ms. Amelia is throwing down in there doing."

Harbor squeezed Cherice's hand and laughed. "Well, good, because we want you to stay, and Ms. Amelia cooked enough food for an army...maybe two."

"Now that's what I wanted to hear because I am hungry," Carlton Ferebee exclaimed as he stepped forward to give Harbor a hug. Before letting her go, he said in a voice loud enough to reach back and grab Ahmad's attention, "If a man knows not what harbor he seeks, any wind is the right wind" – Lucius Annaeus Seneca.

Harbor stepped out of Carlton's embrace and offered the man she affectionately called "Pops" a quizzical glance. "Pops, what does that even mean?"

Carlton walked past Harbor to enter the house. Cherice winked at Harbor, then followed her husband into the house. "It means I got some eating to do, and you got some talking to do with my son," he responded, making determined strides toward the kitchen.

Harbor turned to follow her guests into the house but was stopped by the warm feel of Ahmad's hand on her bare arm. She let his hand slide down her arm and find its way to her fingers.

"Ahmad, I...."

He put his other hand around her waist and drew her to him. "Five minutes."

Harbor sighed. Of its own volition, her head leaned into his chest. "Okay."

Although Ahmad was sure everyone in the house knew he and Harbor needed a minute to talk and would respect their privacy, he closed the door without releasing Harbor from his embrace. He allowed himself the liberty to savor the lavender and lilac aroma he always associated with being in Harbor's presence before he spoke. "I think Pops is right."

Harbor slowly raised her head, so their eyes met. "About?"

"About us," he said. "I'm sure that quote was meant for me. He was telling me in his philosophical way to figure out what I want and to go for it."

"And what is it you want?" She held on to her breath for dear life. "Wait, don't answer that."

Ahmad cocked his head. His locs swaying with the motion. "Come again."

"Let me get this out." Harbor inhaled sharply, then released. "I need to apologize to you for being all weird about Choir Kelly. I was trippin'. I'm sorry."

"Choir Kelly?" Ahmad asked and chuckled. "Is that what we're calling her?"

Harbor groaned. "No, that is just me being...jealous." She hated to admit she *was* jealous of the deceptively beautiful diva. "I saw how Kelly looked at you...how most of the female choir members looked at you. All those biscuits were ready to sop you up like gravy. Like gravy, Ahmad. Gravy."

Ahmad could not help the laughter that bubbled up and out of him. "Tink, only you could pair an apology with a food comparison on Thanksgiving Day." He shook his head. "And you have nothing to be jealous of," he said emphatically. "Kelly and I are *just* friends. And she is good people."

Harbor could neither confirm nor deny the 'good people' statement. But Ahmad had always been a good judge of character, so she would let his friendship with the songbird be whatever it would be. She chose not to spend another minute of her life worrying about something that was nothing.

"Is it alright with you if we forget about Kelly?" He asked seriously.

"Permission granted," Harbor responded. "If I recall, you were about to tell me what it is you want."

Ahmad leaned down to grace Harbor's cheek with a gentle kiss that spoke of more to come. "I want you, Harbor Monae Wilson, and I want us if you will have me."

Harbor wanted to scream an unequivocal "Yes!" Of course, she would have him. She would love him forever and ever. Was he kidding? Before she could fix her lips to finally give herself over wholly and completely to Ahmad, one...no two sets of footsteps walked up the porch and invaded their space.

Harbor did not bother to peer around Ahmad's shoulder to see who their untimely guest was. She could spot the sound of Patrice's standard, Mary Jane shoes with her eyes closed, which they happened to be. She opened her eyes, but instead of acknowledging her sister and brother-in-law's presence, Harbor snuggled deeper into Ahmad's embrace.

"Y'all look cozy," Patrice murmured as she approached Harbor and Ahmad. "No worries. We won't interrupt. But y'all need to move because you're blocking my access to Ms. Amelia's cornbread."

"Exactly," Colin agreed. "We are very hungry people." He placed a hand on Ahmad's shoulder. "It's about time, Man."

Ahmad gave his friend a slight nod, then he and Harbor scooted away from the door.

Before Patrice could turn the doorknob, she and Harbor locked gazes. Patrice sent Harbor a wink that conveyed, "All is well," then walked into the house.

This time, Harbor sighed with relief.

"What was that for?" Ahmad asked.

"Just a little sisterly secret," Harbor responded. "Nothing I can make public."

Ahmad nodded. "I can respect that." He stepped back to create just enough space between them so that their eyes met. "What about us? Is that something you are ready to go public with?"

Harbor stepped out of Ahmad's embrace and threw her arms up in a glorious release. "World, let it be known that I love Ahmad Ferebee!" She yelled with every ounce of love and longing in her soul. "I love this man!"

Ahmad threw his head back in a laugh, then swooped Harbor in his arms. He spun her around the porch in a joyous dance. When he finally placed her down, the kiss they shared was slow and sweet, like he hoped the next phase of their journey would be.

Harbor allowed herself to feel and accept Ahmad's love in a way she had not before, even when they were engaged. At this moment, she felt free to love and to be loved. Instead of worrying about the next minutes and moments of their life, Harbor would fully embrace this beautiful space and allow God to continue to help her trust in His timing and His path for her life.

This whole scene seemed to be a repeat performance of Patrice and Colin's wedding reception as Harbor and Ahmad remained locked in each other's embrace, completely unaware of anything taking place around them. However, this time, there was no uncertainty about where they were going or what they wanted from each other. What they wanted *was* each other.

An hour later, they were seated at a bountiful Thanksgiving table alongside their family and friends. Apparently, her Aunt Francine and Mason had arrived at some point when she and Ahmad were all snuggled up on the porch because Ms. Mills and Mr. Avery were also seated at the table. The love-fog they were experiencing was real because Harbor did not hear either visitor walk up the porch or open the front door to enter the house.

Harbor looked around the table at her family and the new additions that had come into their lives. She marveled at the realization that Ahmad and his parents were once again in her life as a special gift God created just for her.

Although her mother and Mason had only known each other for a short time, Harbor had a feeling their obvious attraction for one another would blossom into something more. At least, she hoped so for her mother's sake. Elizabeth was a vibrant woman and should experience love again. Wow, love after fifty. Harbor was not mad about that.

And if her calculations were correct, they would have a new little ladybug or little fella to dote on this spring. She was so ready to be an auntie. They were so, so blessed.

I am so blessed. Thank you, Lord.

***

After dinner, it was a strictly ladies after party in the parlor. Harbor, Elizabeth, Ms. Amelia, Patrice, and Francine all snuggled up on the sofa or loveseat to watch Christmas movies and polish off the rest of the sweet potato jacks and vanilla bean ice cream.

It was no surprise to Harbor that Patrice ate circles around them all by scarfing down three hefty servings of dessert. Apparently, her baby sister's appetite was back and ready to make up for lost time. Patrice may not have been prepared to spread her joyous news just yet, but the astute women in their circle would soon be able to read between the lines if she kept up her pie-eating-contest pace for much longer.

Patrice may have decided to keep her baby news a secret, but Harbor was ready to explode with news of her own. She wanted to tell all the women she loved to prepare for a wedding because Ahmad had dropped down on one knee and asked for her hand in marriage, during their marathon embrace on the porch.

Even though Harbor wanted to scream her news, which was five years in the making, she decided to take a page out of Patrice's playbook. There was something about holding on to a piece of beautiful, life-changing news for as long as possible before the world had a chance to have its say.

When Harbor stood to take her plate to the kitchen, she caught Elizabeth smiling at her from the other end of the couch. Could she have already figured out Harbor's secret? *No way.* Mama-radar was good but not that good.

Harbor smiled at her mother as she walked down the row of women, collecting empty plates. When she reached her mother, Elizabeth took the plates from Harbor and placed them on a side table. She stood and held Harbor's hands.

"Did I ever tell you how happy I am to have you home?"

Harbor squeezed her mother's hands. "A time or two." She laughed. "What's up?"

Elizabeth winked at Harbor, then picked up the remote and hit the mute button.

Patrice huffed. "Kind of at a pivotal point in the movie, Mom. Will he or won't he get the girl?" She asked with just a bit of sarcasm.

Seated in a side chair with her stocking feet crossed at the ankles, Ms. Amelia blurted, "That boy ain't crazy. I think he will."

At that predicament, everyone laughed.

"I think you are right," Elizabeth agreed. "I just need a moment of everyone's time." She inhaled a long, slow breath, allowing her emotions to stay in check for a while longer. "I am so thankful for each and every one of you. Your love and support have made my life fulfilling in a way I never knew it could be."

"Aw, thank you, Mama," Harbor said and enveloped her mother in a warm embrace. "We love you too."

Elizabeth swiped at a stray tear. "I know you do, Baby. And I know you love this house. That is why I have decided not to sell it."

Harbor could not stop the smile, spreading across her face if she wanted to. And she did not. Even though she'd made peace with the possibility of her mother selling the house, the thought still hurt her heart just a little. "What made you decide not to sell?" Harbor asked tentatively.

Elizabeth smiled at Harbor, then winked at Patrice. The wink Patrice sent Elizabeth's way screamed of a conspiracy. "You, my love. I decided not to sell the house because of you."

"Me?" Harbor pointed to herself in disbelief.

"Yes, but I am moving."

Francine jumped from her seat. "Excuse me, my friend, we never discussed a move. I have only given my stamp of approval for you having a man-friend. Not to move."

"Not out of the area, Franny. Just out of this house. And I do not need your approval to spend my time with Mr. Mason Avery. Thank you very much."

Francine nodded. "Continue."

Elizabeth laughed at her friend. "Thank you." She turned to Harbor. "Amelia and I discussed it. We have decided that our next chapters would be a lot more interesting if we moved into a condo together."

Her mother and Ms. Amelia living in a condo...what? "But what about the house? If you are not going to sell it, then...."

Elizabeth locked eyes with her daughter. "I'm not selling the house because I am giving it to you. It will be here whenever you are ready for it."

Harbor touched her heart. "*Me*? You're giving the house to me?"

Patrice jumped from her seat and walked over to her mother and Harbor. She encircled Harbor's waist with her arm. "Yes, you. Mama and I talked about it. Colin and I don't need the house. It's too big, and I am not about to get caught up in maintaining all this square footage." She laughed. "But you love this house. And it will be here if you decide to ditch Georgia and come home. The Commonwealth welcomes you back with open arms!"

Okay, it was official. The waterworks were in full effect. Harbor did not bother wiping away any of the moisture streaming down her smooth, chocolate complexion. She let the emotional release have its say. She nodded, hugging Patrice first, then her mother. "Thank you. Thank you both."

Francine walked over to join the love fest. "Well, good," she began, "I'm glad I'll still have 137 Briarfield Lane to show up at with my eight-year-old foster son for a visit."

The room fell silent, followed by an explosion of well-wishes for Francine.

"Oh, Auntie!" Harbor and Patrice exclaimed in unison.

Elizabeth grabbed her friend in a fierce hug. "I knew you would get approved."

Francine squeezed Elizabeth tightly. "Thank you, my friend. His name is Niles, and he is such a sweetie. He's been through some hard things for such a little guy. But if all goes well, he will be a part of our lives after the New Year."

Ms. Amelia chimed in, "I always knew you'd make a good mama, Francine. You got plenty of common sense to raise a child up the right way and plenty of love to send them out into the world so they can spread their own joy. I'm happy for you, Girly."

"Thank you so much, Ms. Amelia."

"And don't forget to hop on by the condo when we move. I'll make sure that baby has plenty of my baked treats to munch on." She giggled. "If I'm not entertaining a man-friend of my own."

Francine ran over to Ms. Amelia and gave her a high-five. "Do your thing, Girl."

"Oh, believe me, I will." Ms. Amelia nodded with a sly smile.

After the explosion of good news that spread around their small group like wildfire, the movie and even Ms. Amelia's delectable desserts were long forgotten. The only things that mattered at that moment were their love for each other and moving forward as one.

Harbor could not express how thankful she was to God for bringing her home. He'd restored all that was broken and given her just what her heart needed – a place to land.

8

Epilogue: Six Months Later

Who thought planning a wedding and a baby shower a day apart on Mother's Day weekend was a good idea? Oh, that genius idea fell squarely at Elizabeth's recently pedicured feet. When Harbor and Patrice had double-teamed her the weekend after Thanksgiving at Sunday brunch to inform her that she would soon become a mother-in-law and a grandmother, Elizabeth's joy felt complete. She wanted nothing more than for her girls to experience a lifetime of happiness that exceeded her wildest hopes and imaginations. Elizabeth believed her prayers were coming to pass in ways she could have never envisioned.

Knowing their mother would propel herself into event planning mode, both Harbor and Patrice requested small and intimate events. While the sisters were as different as a full moon from a waning crescent moon, both desired to be surrounded by the loving embrace of only their close family members and friends. Elizabeth recalled Harbor giving her a gentle reminder to, "Keep it simple, Mom. Patrice and I do not want you to go overboard because one or all of us might drown in a sea of tulle. You are too refined of a lady to turn into a Mom-zilla this late in the game. And honestly, that would be tragic."

Harbor's prediction may have been in jest, Elizabeth thought as she sat on the parlor floor, literally surrounded by a rainbow of tulle.

Her girls deserved nothing but the best, and the best is what they would receive. Less than twenty-four hours before Patrice's small list of guests would arrive to celebrate her new arrival, Elizabeth could not decide which combination of colors to use to line the gift bags. Elizabeth Wilson was officially perplexed. That would not do because come rain, shine, or devastatingly wrong mash-up of colors, Patrice's baby shower would go on.

"Mom, you cannot be serious," Patrice demanded from the parlor door. She stood with one hand rubbing the small of her back and the other placed on her rounded, protruding belly. "You told me the gift bags were finished a week ago," she fussed and waddled to the loveseat. "The shower is tomorrow. Tomorrow, Mom."

"I am well aware." Elizabeth stood, offering her child a much-needed hand in making a smooth transition to a seated position. "I have everything under control." Elizabeth resumed her position on tulle island. She picked up one of the pastel pieces and let the fabric live between her hands as she examined it. "Now give me your honest opinion, my love. What color do you think would highlight the yellow undertones in this piece?"

Patrice groaned, which was followed by an unworldly grunt. "Mom, I have no idea," she responded, rolling her neck from side to side. "But since I know that you are not going to let this go, I would say that the purple piece by your foot would look really cute with the green piece in your hand."

Elizabeth looked at her daughter like she was poised to eat a bowl of gazpacho with a salad fork. "I believe you mean chartreuse and violet, dear." She fired off a light laugh, then picked up the section of the violet tulle and paired it with the chartreuse fabric in her hands. "I think you are right about these colors. They are the perfect match, like you and Colin. You always did have a keen eye for fashion."

Patrice huffed. "What I have are swollen feet, a wardrobe full of clothes that refuse to conform to my new curves and a craving for vinegar chips dipped in maple syrup."

"Ew," came the immediate response from both Elizabeth and Harbor.

Elizabeth looked up to see her oldest daughter, gliding into the room with a pep in her step that could only be attributed to her status as a bride. Harbor and Ahmad would commit their lives to each other as man and wife on Sunday. Elizabeth sighed. She was truly blessed.

Harbor plopped down on the loveseat beside her sister. She placed a gentle arm around Patrice's shoulder. "You know that's nasty. Right?" Harbor scrunched up her nose. "Vinegar and maple are not friends."

Patrice flicked her hand at Harbor like she was shooing away a pesky fly. "When you and Ahmad decide to give me a niece or nephew, we'll see how wild your hormones act up."

Harbor threw her head back in a joyous laugh. "Bring it. I cannot wait to have babies with that man."

Patrice eyed her swollen feet. "We'll see."

"We will," Harbor responded. She took a moment to gaze at her mother who sat oddly quiet amid too many conflicting colors. "Mom, I thought you said all of this was done."

"That's exactly what I said," Patrice added her two cents. "This baby shower and wedding are upon us, Mother."

Elizabeth did not respond to either of her girls. The peanut gallery known as Harbor and Patrice had not lifted one finger to prepare for the biggest moments of their lives. Harbor's long-running excuse was that she could not focus on wedding details when she had to move all her things from Atlanta back to her childhood home.

Elizabeth nearly clutched her pearls when she learned that Harbor had found one or two spare minutes to have her final dress fitting.

And Patrice was not any better. Elizabeth's youngest had spent every spare moment nesting to prepare for the arrival of her first-born child. Choosing baby shower games and appropriate finger foods did not make it on Patrice's top ten list of things to do. Elizabeth thanked God she did not have to also worry about packing up and moving out of her home.

When she told Harbor at Thanksgiving she was gifting the house to her, Elizabeth wasted no time in buying a condo with a stunning ocean view for herself and Amelia to enjoy. The two women had moved into their new home the first of the year and left 137 Briarfield Lane for Harbor to do with as she wished. Apparently, her daughter wished to have a wedding by the lake like her sister had done a year earlier. Harbor's wish was finally about to come true. Elizabeth inwardly laughed, then stood.

"Ladies, I am famished. Why don't we leave all of this," Elizabeth did a grand flourish with her hands, "until I am fortified and ready to slay this gift bag madness."

Harbor jumped to her feet. "That sounds good to me. I could go for a burger and fries."

Both Harbor and Elizabeth reached out to offer Patrice a helping hand. Well into her ninth month, standing without assistance was off the table.

As she grasped each of their hands and began to stand, Patrice felt a cool stream of water flowing down her legs. For what felt like an eternity, Patrice gawked at the pool of water forming at her bare feet. Wearing her beloved chunky Mary Jane heels had also become a casualty of pregnancy somewhere around her sixth month.

Patrice exchanged terrified gazes with her mother and then with Harbor. "Oh. My. God. What is this?"

***

By days end of Mother's Day weekend, the Wilson family had pulled off an epic baby shower for Patrice and one of the most unusual weddings Elizabeth had ever witnessed for Harbor and Ahmad. Neither of which included color-coordinated gift bags for their guests, a five-tiered lemon and brown butter wedding cake, or a renowned caterer flown in from Napa, California. All of Elizabeth's carefully thought-out plans landed in a puddle on the parlor floor alongside Patrice's amniotic fluid.

When Elizabeth and Harbor had driven Patrice to the closest hospital, the mother-to-be became oddly calm during the entire drive. Through her rearview mirror, Elizabeth observed Patrice methodically practicing breathing techniques she'd learned from her doula, Trish. The measured inhales and exhales almost calmed Elizabeth's frayed nerves. Almost, but not quite.

Harbor did not fare any better than her mother. Even though they were less than a fifteen-minute drive from the nearest hospital, a jittery Harbor could not calm herself long enough to read the map directions on her phone or enable the voice activation to navigate them to their destination. Thankfully, by the time they'd pulled up to the hospital's entrance doors, thirty minutes later than expected, Colin and Ahmad were waiting to assist the women they loved.

After acknowledging Harbor and Elizabeth with a brief wave, Colin walked over to the car, pushing a wheelchair toward his wife. Colin slid an arm around Patrice's waist as he helped her out of the car. He then leaned down to whisper words that only Patrice could hear, which made her smile. Patrice stood on her tiptoes to kiss her husband, then eased into the hospital-issued mode of transportation.

Admiring the entire scene, Elizabeth did not know if she was witnessing a young couple on the brink of becoming first-time parents or a couple who had weathered many of life's storms and knew the value of cherishing each moment. She knew Colin and Patrice were a match made in heaven, but the sweet sight before her eyes only added confirmation to what she'd seen play out in their relationship since they were juniors in high school.

As Elizabeth handed her keys to a valet, she spied Ahmad enveloping Harbor in a hug, lifting her off the ground. Her daughter's trusty, red sneakers swayed as Ahmad turned his fiancé around in a loving embrace. It did not surprise Elizabeth to see the lover's embrace quickly turn into a smooch session, which Patrice promptly interrupted.

Pointing to her belly, Patrice yelled, "Hey, you two! Stop all that. Save it for the honeymoon. This baby is ready, and so am I. Let's go," she demanded.

With urgency, Colin pushed his wife through the opened double doors. "It's go time, people. Let's do this."

Harbor and Ahmad linked hands and ran to catch up with Colin and Patrice. As they ran through the doors, Harbor yelled back to her mother, "Are you coming, Mom? A once-in-a-lifetime event is in progress. Don't miss out." She laughed, her final words trailing off as the automatic doors closed.

No, Elizabeth would not miss the joy of seeing her baby cradle her first baby. With that in mind, she walked, not ran, to catch up with Harbor and Ahmad. Elizabeth's heart wanted to take off in a sprint to witness the main event, but her knees begged to differ.

***

Imani Marie Wilson-Banks roared her way into the world exactly two hours after they'd arrived at the hospital. The itty-bitty lioness snuggled in her mama's embrace as her proud daddy stood beside the bed, gazing at his wife and new daughter in awe. Colin placed a kiss on Patrice's glistening forehead. "Thank you," he said, barely above a whisper.

Standing by the door, Elizabeth, Harbor, and Ahmad gave the new family several private moments before descending on them in a loving embrace. Harbor was the first to find the words to describe the gravity of the moment. "She's perfect, Sis."

Patrice gazed at the sleeping form in her arms. "She is. Isn't she?" She let her pinky make a gentle trail just at the edge of Imani's chunky caramel cheek. Patrice held out a hand toward Harbor and waited only a moment for her sister to accept it. "I need you to do me a favor, Sis."

Harbor's left eyebrow shot up in a silent question. The last time her baby sis asked her for a favor, she had found herself coming home to stare down her past hurts and fears woven into her relationships with Ahmad and her mother. That favor had resulted in fences being mended and a restoration of hope for the future. Harbor could only guess what twists and turns this favor among sisters would result in.

***

On Sunday, Mother's Day, Patrice's request entailed Harbor and Ahmad moving their wedding ceremony to her bedside. Because of blood loss during delivery, her doctor had informed her that she and Imani would not begin life outside the confines of the hospital until Monday afternoon at the earliest. Patrice knew Harbor would postpone her special day until she was strong enough to walk her down the aisle alongside their mother. So, she had pulled a few strings with some of the hospital staff to transform her temporary accommodations into a makeshift chapel filled with colorful floral bouquets and random balloons, courtesy of the hospital's gift shop.

Ahmad being the kind-hearted man he had always been, agreed to the wonky plan with one make-or-break condition. He'd insisted on having the privilege of dancing with his bride in front of their family and friends, even if that dance took place in a hospital room. Harbor had initially given the idea a hard pass. She was well aware her two left feet took on a life of their own on the dance floor. Harbor's eternal love for Ahmad and her inability to say no to her baby sister were the only factors that propelled her to move forward with Patrice and Ahmad's plan.

After Pastor Ramsey pronounced Ahmad and Harbor as the new Mr. & Mrs. Ferebee, the small gathering of guests watched the groom take his bride to the dance floor. AKA...the foot of Patrice's hospital bed. Mesmerized by the beauty of what she was witnessing, Patrice let the tears freely flow down her face and fall like spring rain onto her hospital gown.

Patrice smiled as she watched her brother-in-law hold onto Harbor who looked ravishing, wearing an A-line lace dress that hit just above her knees. Her sister's ebony mane cascaded in waves down her exposed back with reckless abandon. Patrice had never seen a more beautiful vision.

When she finally allowed her gaze to shift from admiring Harbor and Ahmad, Patrice noticed Colin, standing near a window, away from the subdued but enthusiastic celebration. Her husband cradled their daughter to his chest as if the little one would break if he made one wrong move. This man had already been nominated for and won the Father of the Year award in her eyes. Patrice could not have envisioned a scene that would have brought her greater joy. It was her first Mother's Day, and she was blessed beyond measure to be Imani's mommy. Her life could not get any sweeter.

The End

Thank You

Thank you so much for taking this journey of hope and healing. I hope you enjoyed reading the Briarfield Lane Collection as much as I have enjoyed writing *Coming Home* and *A Place to Land*. Both *Coming Home* and *A Place to Land* can also be enjoyed as audiobooks.

I am currently working on several other projects. Please be on the lookout for other stories that you can fall in love with as soon as I hit the Publish Button!

Also, please consider adding a review. I am so thankful that you have taken the time to connect with these characters! I appreciate you all. I look forward to publishing more stories with characters that inspire me, and I hope will inspire you as well!

With much gratitude,

Stephanie

Milton Keynes UK
Ingram Content Group UK Ltd.
UKHW040254291024
450401UK00005B/18